THE CRACKED REFLECTION

an introductory novella to
REFRACTION

Terry Geo

First Edition

For Ken, always!

CONTENTS

CHAPTER ONE

Kent - 1970

Screaming could be heard coming from the gardens of Braighton Manor. As Lord and Lady Braighton rushed towards the noise, their little girl, Maria, was racing towards them, holding her face as she ran. To her mother's horror, she watched as the five-year-old trampled her prize azaleas, leaving a trail of broken stems and crushed petals in her wake. Lord Braighton scooped up the child and cradled her in his arms.

"What's the matter darling? What happened?"

Through loud cries, the young girl replied. "Mr Piggy punched me in the face and called me a 'filthy bitch'."

Her parents looked at each other in stunned silence as Maria sobbed in her father's arms. Elena stroked her daughter's hair while mouthing to her husband, "what do we do?"

Later that day, Doctor Gayle was in the grand drawing room, talking to the concerned parents. Maria was upstairs with her nanny. Sounds of joyous laughter could be heard emanating from her bedroom; a stark contrast to the atmosphere downstairs, where Lord and Lady Braighton were sitting on the antique sofa, as the maid served them tea.

"Thank you, Hattie. Could you close the door on your way out please?" Lady Braighton asked, softly. The maid nodded and quietly carried the tray out of the room, closing the large, wooden door behind her and sealing off all sound from the outside. The doctor sat forward in the large Chesterfield and regarded the parents. He had known Henry and Elena for many years and had rarely seen them this worried. After taking a sip of his hot drink, he placed the tea cup into its saucer and gently guided it onto the side table.

"It is common for young children to have imaginary friends," he began, "especially when they are an only child."

Lord Braighton ruffled his moustache and cleared his throat before leaning forward to meet the doctor's gaze. He spoke softly, but determinedly. "We're not concerned that she has an imaginary friend, Dick, it's our daughter's imagination we're worried about. This 'Mr Piggy' is a terrible influence. He's violent and extremely corruptive. Earlier today, we found her in the garden, hysterical, covered in mud and crying. One minute she'd been watching the fish in the pond and the next, she was a screaming banshee. Once I'd gotten her to calm down a bit, she told us that her imaginary friend had punched her in the face and called her a bitch."

"A filthy bitch," Lady Braighton interjected.

"Oh, I see. That is concerning. Where would a five-year-old girl pick up such language?"

"Well certainly not from us, and I'm sure none of the staff would say something so foul in our daughter's presence."

"Indeed, but for her to know such a word, she must have picked it up from somewhere. She started school recently, perhaps she heard one of the other students say it?"

"I can't believe anyone at Treefold Primary would speak that way," Lady Braighton replied, defensively. "It's a very respectable school."

The aged doctor crossed his legs and stroked his beard in deep thought. His eyes wandered towards the far end of the room. Floor-to-ceiling shelves, filled with hundreds of books, adorned the walls. "Could she have maybe read the words or heard them from the television or radio?"

"We have a lot of books here, but I can assure you that none of them include such profanity and in any case, she's only just learned how to read." Lord Braighton looked over to the TV cabinet. "As for the television, we rarely watch the darn thing and Maria is in bed by 7pm, so she isn't subjected to the more adult content."

"She used to like 'Watch with Mother'," Lady Braighton added, "but that's not on TV anymore."

"And I suppose there were no markings on your daughter's face to indicate she had been struck?"

Lord and Lady Braighton side-glanced at each other.

Elena looked uneasy as she spoke. "That's just

the thing, doctor. She does have a mark on her face which looks very much like she's been hit."

"Oh right. Do you think she hit herself to give credence to her story?"

"I can't imagine she has the strength," Lord Braighton said, concerned. "She's just a little-bitty thing and although I am proud of her academic abilities for someone so young, I very much doubt she has mastered the art of deception by age five, at least not to this degree."

"Yes, you're quite right Henry, I apologise. If we take Maria, her school and any undesirable media out of the equation, what does that leave us with?" Dick already suspected the answer, he just didn't want to lead with such an accusation. He'd already overstepped his position by pointing the finger at their daughter.

"We have a few ideas but honestly, we don't know for sure. She never leaves the grounds of the manor unaccompanied and we have security personnel on the gates 24 hours a day. The only people she could have access to..." Lady Braighton placed her hand onto her husband's lap to stop him continuing. She was unable to accept, what she assumed, he was about to suggest. The mere thought caused her to start shaking, rattling the cup and saucer she was holding in her other hand.

"What is it you suspect?" the doctor inquired. Do you believe this 'Mr Piggy' to be an intruder, or," he paused a moment before continuing, "perhaps someone who works for you?"

Lord Braighton reached out to steady his wife's shaking hand. "Regrettably, that is where my thought process has taken me, as much as it pains me to believe such a thing. Of course, this is only speculation. We have no proof."

"No Henry. It's not right. I simply won't believe it!" Lady Braighton exclaimed, carefully placing her tea onto the table in front of her. She sat forward and composed herself. "I know every single person in this house and those who work the grounds, I interviewed many of them myself. Most of them live here, some have for decades. These people are our family. They are above suspicion."

"But Elena…"

"No Henry, you have to stop this line of thinking and trust me. There is no way anyone here would ever harm Maria." She released her hand from her husband's grasp and turned towards the doctor. "You may have come to the same conclusion as my husband, doctor, but Henry doesn't know these people like I do. I am the one in the house all day; I spend all of my time with the staff. They are good, honest people. If I had any doubts about their intentions, any at all, they wouldn't be here."

"Of course, I shall trust your judgement, Lady Braighton. I take it then, that you believe this 'Mr Piggy' to be an intruder?"

"Perhaps I would have, if it were not for the fact that I have been with Maria on many occasions while she has been playing with her imaginary friend. For months now, she has been reading to him, playing on the swings or in the sandpit, she even rides her pony with him. Of course, there is no one else there with her, but she talks to him constantly and has full conversations as if he were responding; of which I only hear one side. In the beginning, I felt it was good for her to have a friend and to be honest, I was impressed that our little girl could create conversations using only her imagination. I – we – have longed for a brother or sister for her..." A lump caught in Elena's throat.

Lord Braighton picked up the conversation. "We have tried for more children, but, well, you know the complications we've had." He lovingly placed his hand onto his wife's lap, she placed hers on top of his and gently squeezed.

Dick nodded. The couple had been trying for years to have a second child, but complications from Maria's birth had made it virtually impossible for Elena to conceive a second time. Thousands of pounds had been spent on specialists and invasive examinations, but nothing had worked and now they had resigned themselves to the fact that Maria would always be an only child.

Elena dabbed her moist eyes as the room fell into silence. Dick finished his tea and pondered the information he had just learned. After a moment, he stood up decisively. "With your permission, I would like to examine Maria."

"By all means." Lord Braighton stood up to meet the doctor. "Nanny is looking after her at the moment, in Maria's room."

Lady Braighton led the charge up the stairs and onto the first floor. A corridor of beautifully, hand-crafted, ornate doors lined the wide passageway. At the end of the hall, was Maria's room. The cedar door was covered in hand painted drawings, haphazardly pinned to the wood. This acted as a reminder to the three adults that they were about to enter a child's domain. As Henry walked inside, they were immediately presented with Nanny, laying down on the floor, unconscious. Maria was nowhere to be seen. Doctor Gayle knelt down and checked Nanny's pulse.

"Call an ambulance!"

In a panic, Lord Braighton rushed out of the room as Lady Braighton began calling out for her daughter. Her head darted urgently around the spacious room until she heard muffled sniffling coming from behind the doll's house. There, she found Maria, scrunched up in a ball, quietly crying.

"It's alright my darling, come on out. You're safe now."

Maria slowly crawled from her hiding spot and into the arms of her mother.

"What happened?"

"Mr Piggy did it. He attacked Nanny and said I was next, so I ran over here and hid." Maria buried her head into her mother's chest and sobbed.

Two weeks later, Doctor Gayle was back at the manor.

"I have spoken with your former nanny and she believes she must have tripped over a toy or something. She told me there was no one else in the room except for Maria, who was sitting at her desk at the time, painting. When Maria spilled a jar of water, the nanny had stumbled in her haste to get over to the desk and mop up the mess. As she fell, she hit her head against the chest of drawers and fallen unconscious. It has left extensive damage to the cartilage in her right eye, but she is recovering well."

"Why would Maria blame this on her imaginary friend?" Lord Braighton asked.

"I believe when bad things happen, Mr Piggy is Maria's way of dealing with them. Trauma for anyone can often be difficult to process, especially for children. This is an unknown area of their lives for which they have no frame of reference for. Regarding her previous incident in the garden; instead of being struck, I now believe Maria fell over, injured her face and blamed it on Mr Piggy – the same as when her nanny had fallen. Maria's underdeveloped mind once again blamed this on her imaginary friend."

"That doesn't explain why she would say he called her a..." Lady Braighton paused, struggling to say the words, "a filthy b..."

"I know it's difficult to accept, but Maria must have heard those words somewhere, by someone, at some point. It could have been a passing conversation Maria was not supposed to be privy to. In any case, perhaps it's something you will wish to investigate further."

There was an uneasy pause before the doctor stood up to take his leave.

"Well, I should be getting back to the practice. I have passed your details on to a colleague of mine who specialises in the imaginary friend syndrome. He should call you in a day or two, if not, here is his number." He passed the card to Lord Braighton. "I'd also like to see her again next week, to check on her progress and see what we can do for her."

"You're not going to give our daughter any medication, are you?" Lady Braighton asked tentatively.

"I may prescribe her something to calm the more excitable thoughts. At least in the short term."

"She's only five years old, Richard. We don't want our little girl dependent on drugs."

"I understand your reluctance, Lady Braighton and we can discuss this in detail next week, but there's really nothing to be concerned about. We prescribe these kinds of medications all the time. It may even be that we don't need to go down the medication route at all, depending on how well Maria responds to therapy. The doctor I've recommended," he nodded towards the card in Henry's hand, "is revered for his work with children and has an excellent track record with young patients whose symptoms were once far more severe than Maria's."

"Dick knows his stuff, Elena. He wouldn't steer us in the wrong direction," Lord Braighton offered. Elena nodded, still unsure if this was the right course of action to take for her little girl.

CHAPTER TWO

"Maria. Dinner's ready!" Elena turned to her husband. "I know she can hear me, why won't she answer?"

Lord Braighton pushed his chair backwards, scraping the legs across the stone floor. "I'll get her down here," he said, sternly.

"Be gentle, Henry."

Lord Braighton bounded up the stairs and along the corridor to Maria's room. He banged on the door before walking in, without waiting for a response.

"Maria, your mother has been calling you for dinner and you've..." Her room was empty. He checked her bathroom. Nothing. "MARIA?" He shouted, anger rising in his voice. She wasn't there.

Henry, Elena and a few of the staff searched the house and grounds, but no one had seen her.

"Well, she can't have gone far, the security guards on the gate say she hasn't passed by them and there's no way she's scaled the wall." Lord Braighton was pacing up and down in the drawing room. "Unless she's been up that bloody tree-house again and jumped over the wall. I've told her time and again, that thing is a death trap. I should have had it removed years ago!"

"Sit down Henry, before you wear the floor out."

Lord Braighton huffed as he sank into the Chesterfield armchair. "Why does she keep doing this to us?"

"She's a teenager, this is to be expected. She's rebelling."

"Not under my bloody roof she isn't."

"I think that's the problem. We've spent so many years trying to shield and protect her, she's pushing back. She knows nothing of the world outside."

"We travel, we take her on holiday..."

"But always with us. She has no real friends of her own and knows nothing of the world outside these gates. Now she's old enough to know there is more to life than us and the manor, she wants to experience it. She's always been inquisitive."

"She's only 13, there'll be plenty of time for that later."

"Henry, you're not thinking straight. What were you doing at her age? Were you cooped up here every minute of the day? Did you have a chaperone taking you to and from school? Were you excluded from after-school activities, social clubs and friends' parties?"

Henry stayed stoically silent as he processed his wife's words. Eventually his anger subsided and he relaxed his frown. "No, no I wasn't. I was pretty much free to do whatever I wanted. But that was different. Maria is," he lowered his voice, "special. We do these things to protect her."

"She's also a girl who is very quickly becoming a young woman and wanting to explore the world. Perhaps we went too far and became too protective. We can't keep this stranglehold on her forever, Henry. Her imaginary friend hasn't been an issue for years."

"You know what she went through, what we all went through. We did what was best for her."

Elena reached out and held her husband's hand. "And we need to continue doing what's best for her. We need to allow her to make her own choices. To start making friends, to see the world outside of this place, to have sleepovers with her girlfriends and talk about boys."

Lord Braighton raised his eyebrows.

"Oh Henry," Elena giggled. "She's thirteen – boy talk is to be expected."

"Hmmmph!" Henry slumped in his chair. He wasn't enjoying this conversation, at all.

A noise outside made them both turn their heads to the door as it creaked open. They watched as Maria sheepishly enter the room; her head hung low. "Sorry I missed dinner."

"Where were you?" Henry's voice was stern and sharp.

"We were worried," Elena interjected, hoping to soften the mood.

"I was just out and lost track of time."

"Out? Is that all we're getting? Just, 'out'! Why

didn't you tell us where you were going? What if something had happened to you?"

"Henry!"

"No Elena, it's clear we've been too soft on the girl. We have rules in this house and we all need to abide by them."

"I'm not one of your cadets," Maria mumbled, inaudibly.

"What was that? Speak up, girl!" Henry boomed.

Maria looked up, a deep anger rising inside of her; tears begun to cloud her eyes. A surge of adrenaline-fuelled confidence filled her being as she stood upright, ready to face off with her father. "This isn't the army and I'm not one of your cadets you can push around. I hate it here. I never get to do anything I want to do; only what you want me to do."

Lord Braighton's face turned red with rage. The left side of his face twitched as a deep growl rumbled in the back of his throat. "How dare you! Go to your room!" he bellowed.

Maria opened her mouth to retaliate, but saw her mother shaking her head. Instead, she stamped her right foot on the floor, gave a mock salute and marched out of the room, deliberately stomping onto every stair as she made her way up to her bedroom.

Elena stood in front of her husband to stop him from charging after her. "Calm down Henry."

"But she…"

"What did we just talk about? Did you not hear

anything I said? She's growing up and as her parents, we need to be the adults here. We need to stay calm and think rationally."

"Hmmph!" Henry turned to the sideboard where the half-empty bottle of cognac was singing out to him.

Later that evening, there was a knock on Maria's door. She was in her nightgown, sat up in bed, reading a book. Her anger from the earlier argument was quickly being overtaken by a need for food. She hadn't eaten since breakfast and her stomach kept growling in frustration at not being fed. As she looked up, both of her parents walked in and perched themselves on the end of her bed. Maria's defences kicked in.

"What?"

"We're not here to fight Maria, quite the opposite," Elena spoke softly in hopes of calming down both her and her husband. "We'd like to have a grown-up conversation with you. No shouting, no arguing – just a chat."

Maria looked dubiously at her father. Although he was no longer scowling, she could tell he wasn't completely comfortable with the situation.

"We understand you've been feeling rather trapped lately and perhaps we have been a little overbearing," Elena continued.

"A little?"

Elena ignored her daughter's quip. "Your father and I have discussed it at length and we both think the best thing would be for you to get out from under our wings."

Maria sat up attentively. "How?"

Henry cleared his throat and began to speak. "How would you feel about attending boarding school? I know the Principal of an excellent all-girl's school in Herefordshire. It would mean starting there next term and you'd be studying and living there."

"You could come home on the weekends though, if you'd like," Elena added.

"A boarding school?" Maria repeated quietly, processing the information.

"It would give you a chance to make your own friends and experience life away from home. We love you Maria, we just want to do what's best for you, don't we Henry?"

"Hmmmm, of course, we do; but if this isn't the right fit, we can look for something else."

"I don't know what to say."

"You don't have to decide right now, we can discuss it tomorrow and go into the finer details," Elena smiled.

"It comes with a condition though," Henry announced, "if you go, you must continue taking your medication. Your mother and I won't be there to help you in the event of… an 'episode'."

"Of course. I wouldn't dream of it!" Maria climbed out of bed and hugged her mother. "Thank you so much." She moved to her father. "Thank you, Daddy." Maria's stomach growled as she hugged him.

"It sounds like someone needs supper before bed." Elena looked at Henry, who nodded in agreement. "Come on, let's see what leftovers Hattie has in the fridge."

Arriving at boarding school was emotional, terrifying and exhilarating in equal measures for Maria. Her dorm room was small, but functional. There were two desks, a wardrobe, a chest of drawers and a bunk bed. She chose the bottom bunk while her roommate, Yasmin, was more than happy to take the top.

Wallfern Academy was a well-established and highly acclaimed school; educating children of some of the richest families in the country. Over the three centuries since the boarding school had been founded; celebrities, politicians and even minor Royals had passed through these hallowed halls. Once only accessible to the elite, recent wealth distribution within the country enabled new-money families to enrol their children into the school. This diverse mix of students, at times, clashed with society's more prestigious names.

Maria's first year at Wallfern had been one of the best of her life. She enjoyed her classes, got along with the teachers and made many new friends; including a close bond with her roommate, Yasmin. Everything was going smoothly, until half-way through the second year, when Maria found a hurtful note left in her locker. Initially, she was upset to read the spiteful things someone thought about her and a little embarrassed that this had happened. The note also warned her not to tell anyone about it. Against her better judgement and frightened as to what might happen if she disobeyed, she didn't tell anyone about the note. Not even when a second one appeared in her school bag, or at the end of the year, when a particularly nasty note had been hidden under the pillow on her bunk. The knowledge that the bully had gained access to her room, terrified her into total submission.

When Maria returned home for the summer holidays, her parents thought there was something wrong, but she denied it, blaming her sombre mood on the excess of homework she had been given.

By the time her third year at Wallfern rolled around, the excitement she had once felt for the school had been replaced by fear. Who was this person, why were they leaving hurtful notes and what had she done to warrant them? On her first night back, she had gone to the library after dinner, to finish up some homework. It was late in the evening when she made her way back to the dorm. The lights had been dimmed in the corridor and she didn't see the person walking towards her from the opposite direction. She accidentally collided with another student.

"Oh, sorry," Maria smiled, embarrassed. In front of her stood a broad and tall girl with short cut hair and a sneer on her face. She must have been in a year below, as Maria didn't recognise her at all.

"Watch it, Braighton!" The girl deliberately

pushed past her and disappeared down the hall.

Maria walked back to her room, confused. Who was that and why had she emphasised her surname?

She didn't sleep well that night. Was this the person who had been sending the notes? If it was, why? They didn't even know each other.

The next day, another note was left in her locker, confirming her encounter the previous night had been with the bully. Maria instantly felt a knot in the pit in her stomach.

"Hey, are you ok?" Yasmin touched her shoulder, making her jump.

Maria spun around; she was pale and close to tears.

"What's wrong?"

Maria pocketed the note and closed her locker, carefully scanning the hall. "Come with me."

She led Yasmin into the music store room and proceeded to tell her best friend everything that had happened up to this point.

"Why didn't you tell me before?" Yasmin asked incredulously.

"I was told not to and was scared of making the situation worse. I hoped it just would go away."

"What does that note say?"

Maria passed the folded piece of lined-paper to Yasmin, who read it aloud. "'*If you touch me again, I'll break your scrawny neck.*' Shit!"

"What should I do?"

"You need to tell a teacher."

Maria's hand trembled as she retrieved the

note. She knew Yasmin was right, but once the teachers knew, so would her parents. She was meant to be independent now. If her Mum and Dad got involved, they might say she wasn't ready to live away from home.

"No, not yet."

"What? She's threatened you; you have to tell someone."

"I can't, I need to do this myself. If it gets any worse, then I'll tell a teacher. For now, it's just some stupid notes. I can deal with them, they're just words. Promise me you won't say anything."

"This is serious Maria. What if she physically hurts you?"

"She won't. She just sends these stupid notes. Honestly, I can deal with this. If it escalates, then I'll tell a teacher."

Yasmin wasn't convinced, but promised not to say anything until Maria was ready.

"OK, but you don't go anywhere alone from now on. We need to stick together at all times."

"Thank you," Maria smiled.

Although she had told her best friend she could deal with this herself, the truth was, it was beginning to tear her apart. Sleepless nights were spent worrying about what tomorrow might bring, causing a lack of sleep which began to impact her school work. Her grades began to slip and on occasion, she had even nodded off in class.

One night, as she was staring up at the underside of the top bunk as she did every night, Maria felt a sudden urge to use the toilet. Checking the clock, she noted it was past 2am. Yasmin was fast asleep. She didn't want to wake up her personal bodyguard just for a toilet run. *Who was going to be around at this time anyway?* She snuck out of her room, and tip-toed, barefoot, along the cold, stone floor. She slowly pushed open the bathroom door, careful as to not make a sound as she entered. Once inside, her senses were assaulted by an acrid smell of smoke. As she turned towards the stalls, in front of her were three girls huddled together, smoking cigarettes and passing around what looked to be a bottle of whiskey. At first, everyone was shocked by Maria's presence until the tall girl in the middle moved forward, through the crowd of smoke, revealing herself. It was Maria's bully.

"What are you doing here Braighton?"

"I.. I err, I..."

The girls started laughing as she stammered her words.

"You want to use the stalls?" the bully asked.

Maria nodded warily.

"Tough shit."

"But I..."

"But I, but I..." she mocked. "Go back to your bed and piss yourself for all I care." The bully moved closer, centimetres away from her face. "And if you tell anyone what you saw here tonight..." she grabbed her by the throat. "I'll squeeze the life out of you. You understand?"

Maria murmured, terrified, as the other girls

sniggered. The bully let go of her neck and Maria ran out of the room as fast as she could. Back in her room, she dove under the covers, trembling. That night she didn't sleep at all.

Maria didn't tell anyone what had happened that night, not even Yasmin. Instead, she retreated into herself. She didn't know why she was being targeted, but hoped that by not saying anything, she would avoid any more trouble. For three weeks, there had been no notes and no late-night run-ins with the bully. Maybe it was over. Maybe the bully realised she'd gone too far and decided to stop harassing her. Maria began to relax and that night was the first time she was able to get a full night's sleep.

After gym class the following day, she helped the instructor pack away the equipment from their tennis game. Everyone else had already left the changing room by the time she arrived and so she showered alone. The sound of the door opening didn't startle her, but her bully standing in the middle of the changing room when she finished her shower, did.

"What's wrong Braighton? Not happy to see me?"

"I... I..."

"There's that bumbling Braighton again. Can you not speak? I guess Daddy's money got you into this school, because it was obviously not your brains."

"What do you want?" Maria began to cry as the bully stepped forward.

"This! I enjoy seeing the fear in your eyes. You obviously didn't take my previous cautions seriously enough. Look at you, all alone without a care in the world. I want you constantly looking over your shoulder in case I'm there."

"Why?"

"Because I hate you."

"I haven't done anything to you."

"You're breathing aren't you, that's insult enough – but don't worry, I can fix that." The bully reached into her pocket and was about to retrieve something when loud voices outside the changing room door made them both turn their heads towards the sound. They could hear the instructor having a conversation with another teacher. A sense of relief swept over Maria.

"This isn't over, Braighton." The bully forcibly pushed her backwards, as she hurried out of the room via the side-door, avoiding the teachers. Maria dropped down onto the bench and cried into her towel.

By the time she got back to her dorm, she was in such a state, that it was impossible to hide from Yasmin. Her best friend was adamant that she should now tell a teacher, but Maria was too scared. Yasmin explained that it was far too dangerous and if Maria didn't say something, she would. Reluctantly, Maria agreed to talk to her form tutor in the morning. It was late now and they both needed sleep. As she laid on her bed, she worried about all the possible ramifications. She didn't want to exacerbate the situation, but knew Yasmin was right – it had gone too far. Through sheer exhaustion, Maria eventually fell into a deep sleep.

She was unexpectedly awoken in the middle of the night as a sock was crammed into her mouth and held into position. Panicked and unable to breathe or scream for help, Maria's eyes adjusted to the dark. The leering smile of her tormentor was hovering over her face.

CHAPTER THREE

"Die you little bitch," the bully hissed.

Maria thrashed as best she could, but the girl was much stronger and easily held her down. Freeing one leg, Maria managed to kick up into the bunk above, violently shaking Yasmin awake.

"What's going on?" Yasmin asked, peering down into Maria's bunk, rubbing her eyes. Seeing the shocking scene, Yasmin began to scream and call for help. This spooked the bully, who quickly abandoned Maria and ran for the door – right into one of the arms of one of the teachers, who had heard Yasmin's screams.

"What's going on in here?" the teacher bellowed, quickly grabbing the bully and holding her tight.

Yasmin jumped down from her bunk and attended to her best friend who was still choking on the sock. She yanked it out of her friend's mouth before addressing the teacher. "This girl just tried to kill Maria!"

The morning after, Lord and Lady Braighton were sitting in the Principal's office, holding onto a still, rather-shaken Maria. Miss Haverdome's expression was grave and full of sympathy. After the expected preamble of how unfortunate this isolated case was and how committed they were to the safety of all students at Wallfern Academy; she informed them that the bully's name was Anne Rogers.

"I have had lengthy discussions with both Anne and her mother. From the information I have been able to glean, it appears Anne's father had been an officer in the army and had served under you, Lord Braighton. Do you remember a man named Philip Rogers?"

Henry shifted uncomfortably. "Yes, I do."

Miss Haverdome nodded sombrely. "Anne informed me that her father, along with the rest of his platoon, were killed after being ambushed in enemy territory. I'm afraid, she blames you for his death."

"I understand her wanting to point the finger at the commanding officer, but I assure you, that platoon went against my orders. The area needed a full recon before it was safe and yet..." Lord Braighton stopped himself from getting too emotional and looked over at his daughter. "What does any of this have to do with Maria?"

"When Anne joined Wallfern and learned that your daughter attended the school, she hatched a plan to make Maria's life as miserable as hers had been after her father's death." Miss Haverdome continued, cautiously. "At first, it was a series of hurtful notes, but as the months went on, Anne's need for misplaced revenge kept pushing her to go further."

"And almost killed our daughter!" Henry raged.

"Oh Maria, you poor thing. Why didn't you tell

us this was going on, or at tell Miss Haverdome?" Elena clung tight to her daughter.

"What happens now? Are the police going to be involved?" Henry asked.

"That would be for you to decide. Anne denies attempting to kill your daughter, insisting that she only intended to scare Maria last night."

"Rubbish. The poor girl couldn't breathe. If it hadn't been for her friend…"

Maria began to shake at her father's words, unnerved by the terrifying images constantly replaying in her mind.

"I agree with you Lord Braighton, it went too far. That said, she is a minor and would likely be let off with a caution. I have expelled her from Wallfern and her mother has said Anne will receive any and all help she needs to get better. She's promised to keep me apprised of her progress."

Henry turned to his wife, pouting. He wasn't convinced this was the right course of action.

"Do you think that will work?" Elena asked.

"Anne's mother was shocked and saddened by her daughter's behaviour, she had no idea any of this was happening. She assures me that outside school, her daughter is a kind and loving child."

"Bah!"

Everyone turned to look at Lord Braighton who had folded his arms across his chest, looking increasingly unhappy with the situation.

"I understand your frustration, Lord Braighton. We've never had an incident like this before and

I'm only suggesting what I think is the right course of action. If you believe we should call the police in, I am more than happy to co-operate."

Henry breathed deeply, his face turning redder by the minute, he grunted a few times, but no actual words came out. It was Elena who spoke. "I think it's best if we had some time to digest what you've told us. We're taking Maria home with us today, I think she needs her own bed for the time being. We'll talk about it as a family over the weekend and get back to you, if that's alright?"

"Of course, take all the time you need," Miss Haverdome said comfortingly.

Maria who was still too shaken up to say anything during the meeting, suddenly felt elated at her mother's words. She didn't have to stay at the school tonight! That weekend, the family had lengthy discussions on the best course of action, eventually opting for Miss Haverdome's plan – against Henry's better judgement. He begrudgingly agreed that Maria should have the deciding vote. Even after everything that had happened, she simply wanted to move on with her life.

Maria tried returning to Wallfern the following week. After fending off a barrage of questions about 'that night' from other students, she quickly made her way to the dorms. She was alone when she walked into her old room, stopping in front of her bunk and staring at the freshly made bed. A torrent of disturbing images flooded her conscious mind as she relived her destressing ordeal. She remembered the feeling of cotton expanding and filling her mouth, her eyes opening and focusing in absolute terror as she saw Anne hovering above her face; glaring at her as she clamped her hand down over her mouth. The cold, menacing smile her attacker wore as Maria desperately struggled to breathe – fighting for her life.

She awoke in the infirmary. Maria had collapsed in her room after a suspected panic attack. This was to be the first of many. The violent memories were too difficult to repress, she could no longer sleep in her bed and the torment of that night eventually forced her out of the school. Although it was painful saying goodbye to her friends, especially Yasmin, she knew this was something she needed to do. Maria left Wallfern, midterm, and enrolled in a private day school which was much closer to the manor. As a way to protect herself from this ever happening again, Maria decided to change her family name on the school's register. With the agreement of her parents and the head teacher at Rosewood High, she was now known as Maria Bee.

After three months, she was still the relatively unknown girl who sat in the back of the class and kept her head down. She made a few acquaintances, but feared that, by getting any closer to people, she would expose who she really was. The events at Wallfern had scarred her and as unlikely as it was to ever happen again, there were still 29 other men who had died under her father's command and any one of their children could harbour the same hatred for her as Anne had. She couldn't allow that to happen again. Her parents had tried to ease her worries by explaining this was an isolated incident, but Maria wasn't about to take that chance.

This unfortunately brought with it a new problem; to keep her identity hidden, she had to isolate herself. Even throughout her torment at boarding school, she still had friends. Now she had no playmates, no study-buddies, no one. She was all alone and that ate her up inside – not that it was something she would ever admit to her parents.

Maria opted to walk home every night. The school wasn't too far from home and felt if people saw a Rolls-Royce dropping her off and picking her up every day, it might make them question who she really was. Being a sheltered child in her youth and away at boarding school for her teenage years meant no one knew that she lived in the manor down the road. Here, she was Maria Bee and that's how she intended to remain.

At first, she would walk home via the winding, country roads, but soon discovered a shortcut through an overgrown woodland area. With no clear path, this wasn't somewhere many people frequented, which meant it was the perfect place for Maria to release her frustration. The pent-up anguish, the pain of the past few years and the torment of isolation was too much for the 16-year-old. A fallen log, hidden by deep undergrowth and out of sight from the road, had been a place she would sit and let her tears flow, soaking into the aged bark beneath her. This was her time to vent to the world before dusting herself off and returning home, giving no hint of her deep-rooted unhappiness. Although unconventional, this seemed to work for Maria. A place she could scream, curse and cry if she wanted to. This was her safe space and she was thankful for it. That was until two weeks ago.

After a particular gruelling and lonely day at school – picked last in gymnastics, being left out of the after-school activities and being brushed off by one of her acquaintances – she had needed her safe space more than ever. When she arrived, she was sure she saw someone else sitting on her log. This overgrown part of the woods had no clear path and wasn't frequented by anyone other than herself, yet the closer she got, she was sure there was someone there. Through the thick, overgrown bushes, she squinted. Was it a person? Careful not to get too close and alert them of her presence, she waited to see if the shape moved. That's when the laughter began. It was distant at first, but soon got closer and frightened Maria. She quickly turned around and made her way home before being spotted.

The next day, she cautiously entered her overgrown haven, but the same shape was there again. On the third day, she managed to get a little closer, making a gap in the branches of an overhanging tree. She couldn't see anyone, but she could hear the same laughter. It seemed to be moving closer towards her, sounding clearer than it had been before. Goosepimples ran up her arms and as she turned to leave, her foot caught on an exposed root causing her to fall, face first into the muddy leaves. Laughter. An insane, almost unreal giggling echoed in her ears, raising the hairs on the back of her neck. She picked herself up and ran back home as fast as she could, careful to change out of her dirty clothes before her parents noticed. Since then, she had avoided the woodland area completely, taking the longer route along the country lanes. Her safe space was no longer safe.

CHAPTER FOUR

The school's Summer Dance was held on the last Friday of the school year and was compulsory for all students to attend. As much as Maria protested, there was no getting out of it. She tried to feign a cold, but her mother saw through her ruse.

"Maybe this is exactly what you need. With Yasmin and her family going to Italy, you should make some new friends for you to spend time with over the summer."

"Mum, we are not having this discussion again!" Maria retorted defensively. "How do I know who to trust? That girl tried to kill me. You weren't there, you weren't being held down, unable to breathe or call for help." Maria fell onto her bed shaking, trying to calm down. She tilted her head back, pulling her long hair away from her face.

Lady Braighton sat down next to her. "I know you had it rough at boarding school, darling, and I can't imagine what you went through, but things are different here. Not all people are cruel and not everyone has served under your father you know."

"A lot of people have though. 30 people were killed in that attack, what if all of those families blame Dad? I can't risk it and I can't understand why you don't get that?"

"I do. I'm sorry darling, I'm only trying to help."

"I know Mum, but honestly, you've got to stop pushing me. I know you're concerned, but I can get through this. I just need time to figure out how to be Maria Bee and not Maria Braighton."

Elena pulled back her daughter's hair and began to brush it. "That nasty bully was misdirecting her loss and anger onto you. At least she's getting the help she needs now. I'm just so sorry you had to go through all that. Wallfern has such a good reputation, I'm still shocked this happened."

"I don't blame you Mum; I don't even blame Dad. If anything, I blame myself for not speaking up sooner."

"The blame falls squarely on Anne, not you darling. You have nothing to berate yourself over."

Maria wasn't convinced. After moving schools and having more time to herself, she had been able to reflect on her past. She didn't want to feel weak and helpless anymore. She needed to stand up for herself and not turn to her parents at every stumbling block.

"I'm sure you'll soon start to fit in at this new school," Elena spoke cheerfully. "Once you've made a few friends who you trust, maybe then you can open up about who you really are. They might think it's really cool that you live in a manor."

"Mum! Please, don't ever use the word 'cool' again! It sounds so weird coming from you." Maria laughed, despite herself.

"At least I made you smile." Elena stopped brushing her daughter's hair. "Try and enjoy tonight, please - for me. I've hated seeing you so upset when you come home from school these past few weeks."

Panic surged through Maria; she thought she'd been so careful as to not show her true emotions, but without her safe space, she must have been bringing them home with her. Elena looked at her lovingly. "A mother knows. I haven't asked you about it as I didn't want to embarrass or upset you any further, but please know, you can come to me with anything. I know the adjustment period must be difficult for you and I can only imagine how delicate you feel."

"I'll be fine. I'm not a wilting flower, Mum," Maria responded, resolutely.

"I know you're not. You're a Braighton – whether you choose to disclose that or not. We can get through anything." She smiled warmly. Maria could see the love and concern in her mother's eyes. "I just wish you'd give these new classmates a chance," she continued. "I know you miss Yasmin, but maybe there's someone just as amazing as Yasmin waiting to be your friend. You'll never know if you don't try."

"Maybe you're right, but honestly, for the time being, I'm fine," Maria lied. This conversation was making her feel incredibly uncomfortable and she hated seeing her mother so earnest. "Only two more years of school and I'll be an adult, able to make my own way through life."

"Two years can be a long time without friends sweetie." Elena stood up and walked towards the wardrobe, where a bedazzled, silver gown with exenterated shoulder-pads was hanging. It sparkled as she retrieved it and showed it to her daughter.

"Why don't you try it on and see how it fits."

"It was tailored, Mum; I know it fits. I just don't see why I can't wear something else. That's far too glamorous for a school dance. What about the summer dress I wore for the garden party last year?"

"You've grown since then darling. Humour me. I'm sure, once you put on the gown and we've styled your hair – maybe added a little make-up – you'll look like the belle of the ball."

Maria groaned internally. If she had to go, she'd rather be wearing something simple and preferably dark so she could blend in to the back of the gymnasium, where no one could see her. This garish gown was going to shine an unwanted spotlight on her.

"Oh, and Charlie will be driving you to and from school. People will think it's a hired car or something."

"No Mum, absolutely not! I'll wear the dress as long as I can take a taxi." Maria said, panic rising in her voice.

"Oh, well ok, if you think that would be for the best." *She may be 16, but she still falls for my reverse psychology*, Elena thought with a wry smile.

The dress had done exactly what she'd feared. Arriving late in the hopes of not attracting too much attention, had the opposite effect. As she walked into the crowded hall, flashing disco lights hit the mirror ball, illuminating her entrance. The dance floor was busy, with many of the students moving excitedly to Kids in America by Kim Wilde. As they spun around, several people stopped dancing and pointing in her direction; murmuring to each other and gesturing to more people to look at her. A few girls she'd never spoken to complimented her on the dress and a group of the boys wolf-whistled. It was so embarrassing. Tables at the side of the room had been set up with soft drinks, manned by members of the faculty to make sure no 'incidents' took place. With her head hung low, she quickly made her way to where her favourite teacher was standing.

"Maria, is that you? What a stunning dress."

"Thank you, Miss." Maria replied meekly.

"What's wrong?"

"This," she indicated the dress she was wearing, "was my mother's idea. She thought it would look nice."

"Well, she wasn't wrong, you do look beautiful in it."

Maria could feel the heat rising in her cheeks. "Yeah, thanks. Could I get a coke please?"

"Oh, I don't think that's a good idea."

"Why not?" Maria questioned.

"Your dress. If someone knocks into you, it could leave a stain. Maybe you should have a lemonade instead."

Maria rolled her eyes. She knew this dress was

a bad idea. *Why did I allow Mum to persuade me to wear it? Just smile, get the drink then sit in the corner. You can leave after an hour*, she thought to herself. "Good thinking, lemonade sounds great. Thanks Miss." Maria forced a smile as she took the drink and turned around to scan the room for a vacant chair. Standing in front of her was a group of people huddled together, whispering and looking her way. They quickly dispersed, but a wave of nausea passed through Maria's stomach. She suddenly felt light-headed.

"Hey, are you ok?"

Maria turned around to see Talik, the captain of the rugby team, standing by her side. He was shorter than she remembered, but then recalled she was wearing heels, which slightly elevated her. She had noticed Talik – many times – around school, but he'd never seemed to take an interest in her.

"I'm ok…" she said warily.

"It looked like you were going to fall over."

"Oh." Maria looked down, trying to think of what to say. *People are looking at me and I feel like throwing up – probably not the best thing to tell the boy you fancy,* she thought. "I guess I'm just not used to heels."

She was actually very accustomed to wearing high-heeled shoes. She hadn't wanted to wear them tonight, but tonight wasn't about what she wanted. Her mother had rammed the designer pumps onto her feet before bundling her off in the taxi earlier. They were brand new and rubbed a little on her ankles, but nothing she wasn't already used to.

"Why don't you come and sit down?" Talik offered.

"You mean, before I collapse onto the floor and make a bigger fool of myself than I already have?"

"Why'd you say that?"

Maria indicated the dress she was wearing.

"Are you kidding? You look like a knockout."

"But everyone's staring at me," she whispered.

"Trust me, that's a good thing!" he whispered back, grinning from ear-to-ear.

They walked to the back of the hall where the light wasn't as bright. Giggling girls and boys with approving looks, gestured to them as they took their seats.

"I feel so stupid. Everyone else is wearing casual clothes. I feel like Cinderella, complete with pumpkin coach."

"Seriously Maria, you look beautiful. Everyone's just jealous."

Maria frowned. "I didn't know you knew my name."

"Have you not seen me smiling at you every day since you started here?"

"No!" Maria replied in shock. The truth was, every time Talik had looked at her, she would turn away, embarrassed to be caught staring at him. She knew he was in the year above her and so had different classes and probably different interests from her. He was just a fantasy; she had no idea he felt anything for her, at all.

"I've been hoping to get some time alone with you."

"And you chose tonight, when the whole school is looking at us?" She indicated to the groups of people, still mingling around in their vicinity. Maria hung her head again, embarrassment overtaking her body.

"Hey, don't pay any attention to them." He reached into his pocket and pulled out a hip flask, careful to keep it hidden from prying eyes.

"Do you want some?" he whispered.

"What is it?"

"Vodka, so no one will smell it on you. Should relax you a little bit as well."

Although only 16, Maria had drunk alcohol a few times in the past. Bucks Fizz on Christmas morning, port on Boxing Day, the odd glass of champagne at a family function. Nothing to the point of inebriation, but she was no stranger to it. Spirits on the other hand, were something she had not yet sampled. Her father was an avid cognac connoisseur, but vodka, wasn't that made from potatoes? *How bad can it be if it's made from a vegetable? I eat chips all the time!*

"Sure, but not too much." Maria held out her white-plastic cup of lemonade.

Talik, dropped a small amount of liquid into the glass. It bubbled momentarily before settling down. Maria took a sip and then downed the glass. It was dry and bitter, but not the worst thing she'd ever tasted, suddenly remembering the Foreign Secretary's luncheon last summer – monkey brains. Yuk!

"Wow! You drank that fast. I'll grab you another lemonade."

The night went smoother after a few shots of vodka. She found that Talik was a good conversationalist and he even persuaded her to dance for a short while. She was smiling and felt happy, if a little fuzzy. When the dance finished, Maria wanted to get a cab, but Talik insisted on escorting her home instead. Bowled over by his chivalrousness, she agreed. They talked, they laughed and for the first time in a long time, she felt relaxed. Talik was a joker, he found humour in almost everything and his laughter was infectious.

They slowly walked through the park, and as they reached the boundary of Braighton Manor, Maria stopped at the wall, ready to bid Talik goodnight. He was smiling at her. She smiled back. He leaned forward and Maria's heart began to race. He wanted a kiss. Her first kiss. Without giving it a second thought, she touched her mouth to his. Maria was awkwardly pushed up against the brick wall as the boy bore down on her. The kiss was sloppy and to Maria's horror, Talik kept sticking his tongue out as if it were a lolly she was meant to suck on. She instinctively moved her head to the side, so that his next advance hit her cheek.

"What's wrong babe?" he asked, pouting his red, slick lips.

"I'm just nervous someone might see us, is all." Talik looked around. They were in parkland with no houses around and in front of them was a two-metre-high red-brick wall. "It's the middle of the night and no one lives around here. I doubt any dog walkers are in the park this late."

Not meeting his eyes, Maria responded meekly. "I live here."

Talik laughed. "What, you live out here in the park? Are you a fairy or something? Or maybe a tree nymph?" This really tickled him, making his laughter rise in volume.

"Shush, they might hear you." Maria scolded causing Talik to pause and look quizzically at her, then began laughing again.

"Don't tell me, your pixie parents are here to drag you back to their mushroom?"

Moron! Maria thought and quickly locked lips with him again, instantly shutting him up. When she pulled away, he rubbed the sleeve of his jacket across his mouth.

"Come on then, where is this house of yours?"

Maria was momentarily mesmerised by the amount of salvia this boy was producing – or maybe it was hers? This was her first kiss – was this normal? "You don't expect me to believe you live here, do you?" He motioned to the front gate of Braighton Manor.

Maria shrugged. "This *is* where I live."

"No way! Really? I thought it was a stately home or something."

"It is a stately home."

Talik moved towards the front gate. "You know what I mean, like a museum or something."

"Don't get too close, someone will see you."

Talik, wasn't listening, he was still trying to ascertain if Maria was telling the truth. He stopped at the golden plaque by the side of the gate. "Nice try, but this is Braighton Manor and your surname is Bee."

"I changed it when I joined the school."

"Why would you do that?"

"Long story, now please, come back over here. The last thing we want is for my Dad to see us."

Talik's playful smile suddenly dropped. "You're being serious, aren't you?"

Maria sighed. "Yes, but please don't tell anyone at school. It causes more problems than I can handle." Tears started to well in her eyes.

Talik could tell Maria was genuinely upset. "Of course, I won't tell anyone." He held her gently for a moment, before being drawn back to the manor. "Look at the size of it though. It must be so cool living in a place like this."

"Talik, please. Come away from the gate."

"Do you have servants and stuff?"

Suddenly the security lights came to life, illuminating the grounds and shining a bright, white light directly onto Talik. He instinctively turned his head away to shield his eyes.

Panic rushed through Maria. She grabbed Talik's sleeve and pulled him away from the gate, pinning them both up against the wall, frozen in place. Her heart pounded wildly as she held her breath.

"MARIA, IS THAT YOU?"

Her father's voice boomed across the grounds and rang in her ears. Maria was shaking. She was late home, had been drinking and had possibly been seen kissing a boy outside the walls of her family home. Her body began to convulse and she felt a tightness grip her chest. She slid down the wall, hitting the grass beneath her, tears flowing from her eyes.

"Hey, are you ok?"

Maria was panting, unable to speak, which frightened Talik.

She knew she was having a panic attack. They had become commonplace over the past few months. It didn't make them any easier to deal with though. In an attempt to steady herself, she breathed in slowly through her nose and out through her mouth, just as her doctor had told her to do. But as the gates began to creak open, panic surged through her body like an electrical current and she crumpled, almost unconscious, onto the ground. Talik's eyes widened as he himself began to panic, not knowing what to do.

"I'll go and get help."

"No!" Maria tried to say, but the word was lost. Through tear-soaked eyes, laying on her side, she watched as Talik made his way to the entrance of the Manor. Unexpectedly, he swerved to the left and cracked his head on the corner of the gate, falling to the ground with a heavy bump, blood pooling around him. The last thing Maria remembered, was hearing a high-pitched, maniacal laughter.

"Piggy," she breathed, before passing out.

CHAPTER FIVE

"...can you hear me?"

Maria woke up groggily. As her eyes slowly opened and began to focus, she could see a man hovering over her, shining a torch into her eyes.

"Where am I?" she asked.

"You're in an ambulance on the way to the hospital. My name's Jack, I'm a paramedic," he said gently.

"We're here as well darling."

Maria slowly turned her head to see her concerned parents looking on.

"Do you remember what happened tonight?" Jack asked.

"I think I had a panic attack and passed out." Maria swallowed hard; her mouth was dry.

"Would you like some water?"

Maria nodded and the paramedic held a bottle to her lips, allowing her to sip the drink through a straw. As the liquid ran down her throat, she closed her eyes and began to drift off again.

"She's rather dehydrated," Jack informed her parents. He tapped the IV bag that was currently connected to her arm.

"Will she be alright?" Henry asked.

"I'll recommend that she's kept on the IV when we get to the hospital, we should be there in a few minutes."

Maria drifted in and out of consciousness until they arrived at the hospital and the doors opened, banging onto the sides of the vehicle and rousing her from her sleep.

"If you could just wait outside, please, so we can pull the stretcher out," Jack said to the worried parents.

"We'll just be outside, Maria," Elena smiled, lightly touching her daughter's arm.

Jack adjusted the stretcher before leaning over to whisper to Maria. "Did you have anything to drink tonight?"

"What?" she asked groggily.

"I didn't want to ask you in front of your parents, but I will need to know before passing your charge to the nurses. Did you have any alcohol tonight?"

Maria opened her eyes fully, apprehensive to answer. "Only a little vodka, but not a lot."

"That's alright, thank you for being honest with me." He made a note on the chart.

"What happened to Talik?" she asked, as quietly as she could.

"Was that the boy who was with you?"

Maria nodded.

"He was taken in a separate ambulance, I can ask the other team for an update and let you know later, if that's ok?"

Maria smiled. "Thank you," she said, before closing her eyes again.

Jack clipped the chart to the front of the bed and pulled the stretcher out of the ambulance.

It was morning when Maria awoke again. A steady beeping echoed throughout her sparce, magnolia-painted room. She was encased in layers of starchy sheets making her feel hot and sticky. A gentle breeze coming in from the open window behind her was a welcome respite. She yawned and stretched out, pulling at the blankets and freeing her feet and arms.

The door opened. Henry walked in with a newspaper tucked under his arm and a plastic cup in his hand which he was precariously balancing to keep the steaming contents inside from overflowing.

"Ah, you're awake, how are you feeling?" He urgently placed the drink and paper down on a small table, spilling some of the hot liquid onto his hand. He swore under his breath as he moved over to the bed. As he neared, Maria could see heavy bags under his eyes.

"I'm ok thanks Dad. Have you been here all night?"

"We didn't want to leave you," Henry smiled. "I sent your mother home around 2am as she kept falling asleep in the armchair. I told her I would stay with you and call her later with any news."

"Thank you, Daddy. Where did you sleep?"

Henry indicated the uncomfortable looking wooden chair in the corner of the room. Maria gave him a pained expression.

"I've slept in worse places. The army toughens you up."

Tears filled Maria's eyes.

"Now, now. Don't cry. You're safe, that's all that matters. I can nod off in front of the fire later, don't worry about me."

"I'm sorry Daddy, I feel so stupid."

"There's nothing to feel stupid about." Henry sat on the edge of the bed and held his daughter's hand. "What actually happened last night?"

"I went to the dance and everyone was looking at me, I felt so embarrassed, but this boy - Talik – was nice to me. He made me feel comfortable."

"Hmmmmm," the Lord muttered.

"Not like that Daddy, he was very chivalrous. He offered to escort me home, but I started to panic when we got to the gates as I didn't want him to tell anyone where I lived or who I was. I could feel my chest tightening and I collapsed…" she squeezed her eyes closed, fighting against her emotions. "What happened to Talik? Is he ok? He was worried about me and ran to get help but I remember seeing him fall down."

Henry stroked his moustache, unsure of how much information to divulge. "He hit his head on the gate… pretty hard." He saw his daughter's eyes widen and her breath quicken. "But the ambulance was there within minutes and I'm sure he's doing well."

Maria calmed down slightly. "Is he here? Can I

see him?"

"Not right now sweetheart," Henry quickly responded. He stroked his daughter's hair. "Let's get you better first and then we'll see about Talik."

"But I'm fine now, it was just a panic attack."

"We'll let the doctors do the diagnosing," Henry kissed her forehead. "Will you be alright in here on your own for a few minutes? I need to call your mother and tell her you've woken up. I'm sure she'll be waiting by the phone to hear from me."

Maria nodded. "Say hi from me."

Henry gave his daughter a reassuring smile, which faded as soon as he left the room. He really hoped the boy was ok, but there had been so much blood on the ground. He was still unconscious when the ambulance took him away. Henry nervously walked over to the Nurses' Station to check on his condition.

"Montridge Hospital, please hold. Montridge Hospital, please hold. Montridge Hospital, yes, I'll put you through now. Montridge Hospital, please hold."

Henry waited patiently for the only nurse manning the desk to pause from answering the telephone. As she put down the receiver, Henry cleared his throat. The nurse didn't look up. He decided to be a little more direct. "Hello, Jane," he read from the plastic name tag fastened to her uniform, "my daughter has just woken up. Would it be possible to get a doctor to see her please?"

The nurse sighed, obviously not thrilled

about being interrupted. "Which room?" She asked brusquely, her head still buried in the stack of papers in front of her.

"Room 7. Maria Braighton."

The nurse's head shot up as she regarded Henry, slack-jawed. "You're Lord Braighton."

"I am." Henry furrowed his brow.

"Sorry sir, we're extremely short-staffed today and I haven't had time for my... sorry, I'm waffling. They've been patching calls through from reception and... sorry, I'll check now." The nurse frantically searched through the papers on her desk until she found Maria's charge sheet and paged the doctor assigned to her. The last thing she wanted to do was upset a major benefactor of the hospital.

"The doctor will be down in the next few minutes sir, he's just on his rounds. Is there anything else I can help you with?" The phone began to ring again. Annoyed, she picked up the receiver and slammed it back down, abruptly ending the call. "They'll call back if it's important," she grinned.

"Yes, there is actually." Henry moved closer to the desk and lowered his voice. "There was a boy found unconscious next to my daughter last night, he was taken away in a separate ambulance. My daughter would like to know his condition."

"Of course, sir, if you'll just bear with me. Do you have a name?"

"Only his first name, Talik. He'll be 16 or 17 years old and he was picked up from outside Braighton Manor."

The nurse nodded.

Henry paced in front of the Nurses' Station as she made a few phone calls.

"Henry!" A loud, booming voice made the Lord spin around on his heels as he saw a short, middle-aged man charging towards him. "I thought you were in the building," he declared, with a beaming smile.

"Rajesh!" Henry regarded the pristine, white uniform and returned the smile. "You're a doctor here?"

"Indeed I am. When I saw Maria's name on the patient list, I assumed it was your daughter. There aren't too many Braightons in the area."

"We're an elite breed."

The two men chuckled as they hugged one another.

"I haven't seen you in years. I didn't even know you were back in Kent."

"About six months now," Rajesh replied.

"Why haven't you been in touch?"

"Still settling in old man. I've been meaning to call on you, but work… well, you know."

"I do. You must come over for dinner soon. I'm sure Elena would be chuffed to see you again."

"How is the lovely Lady?"

"She good, well, apart from the obvious."

"Ah, of course, and how is Maria? I haven't seen her since she was a baby."

"Isn't that your area of expertise? I'm hoping you can tell me." Henry looked over to the desk where the nurse was nodding towards him. "She's in room 7," he said to the doctor, pointing down the corridor. "I'll give you some space while you examine her."

"Aye, aye Captain," Rajesh responded with a salute.

Henry watched his old friend enter Maria's room before stepping back towards the nurse. She had a concerned look on her face.

"Did you find him?"

"I did sir, he was taken to Intensive Care." The phone rang again. The nurse muttered inaudibly under her breath before unplugging the cord to the phone, instantly silencing it. Her grumpy expression changed back to one of concern as she looked up at the Lord. "They had to perform emergency surgery to relieve the bleeding on his brain and were working until the early hours of the morning, but I'm afraid he didn't make it."

"He's dead?" Henry said, incredulously. "How could a bump on the head cause him to die?"

"I'm so sorry sir, but that's all I know. I did try to find out more details, but the ICU is incredibly busy at the moment. I can check back later if you like?"

Henry paused for a moment as he tried to process the information. "No. Thank you," he mumbled while walking across the hall and dropping down onto a brown, plastic chair outside his daughter's room.

How am I going to tell Maria? he thought. Henry

felt a pang of emotional pain hit him in the chest.

"She's doing well. I'd just like to run a few more tests, but I'm happy to release her into your care later today." The doctor looked at Henry before sitting next to him. "You ok, Braighton?"

Henry paused for a moment, before turning to his old friend. "Sorry, I didn't get much sleep last night and I'm not as young as I used to be. That's great news about Maria. How does she seem?"

"Physically, she's in fine shape, but emotionally, I think the events of last night have rattled her. I'm recommending a course of therapy to help with the panic attacks. Has she had them before?"

Henry nodded, slowly. "She's had a pretty rough time of it over the past few years, I can tell you. Bullying at her old school seems to have triggered the attacks, but nothing as bad as last night. You remember Rogers? His daughter was a student at the same boarding school as her and took her pain out on Maria. She almost killed my poor girl. It's affected her so badly, she's now scared to even tell people she's a Braighton, convinced this could happen again."

"That's terrible, Henry and totally unjustified. What happened with Rogers and the rest of that platoon was a regrettable tragedy, but it wasn't your fault. You didn't even know the platoon had gone until it was too late. You were cleared at the tribunal; they must have known that."

"Dark times," Henry stated, deep in thought. "It was a senseless tragedy, one which this girl blames me for and as the commanding officer, I can shoulder that blame – but this has nothing to do with Maria and I will not excuse her reasoning for attacking my innocent daughter. We had to move her out of there and into a school closer to home. She's really taken it hard, even changing her surname so people don't know who she is." Henry shook his head slowly. "Our GP prescribed some new medication for her which seemed to be working and I hoped that would be an end of it, but then this happened."

Doctor Sharma looked through Maria's notes. "Yes, I saw that she's recently started a new course of drugs… and how long has she been taking Chlorpromazine?"

Henry thought for a moment. "Must be ten years now."

"But she doesn't have bi-polar or early signs of schizophrenia. At least, there's no mention of either on her chart."

"No, nothing like that. It was prescribed because of the hallucinations she was having of her imaginary friend."

"Lots of children have imaginary friends."

"Not like his one, it was affecting her mental health. Dick, our GP, said this was the best way to treat her. She started on a low dose, but it was increased a few years back after a rather troubling episode on her tenth birthday. The clown we'd hired for the party had been drinking or had taken something before the performance and passed out, head-first, in the cake, almost suffocating on the frosting. It was an accident of course, but Maria was in hysterics, certain her imaginary friend had tried to kill the clown. For weeks she was in a frightful state, until Dick upped her medication."

"I see."

Henry noticed the concerned look on his friend's face. "Why do you ask?"

"I don't agree with this, Dick, was it? I understand he wanted to control the hallucinations, but this is strong stuff for someone so young. Added to that, the medication Maria was given a few months ago can degrade the effectiveness of Chlorpromazine over time and in rare cases, it can completely negate the effects of both medications. For this reason, it's not a combination I advise and certainly wouldn't prescribe to a patient myself."

"Really? Do you think this has anything to do with what happened last night?"

"It's certainly a possibility. If you're comfortable with moving her care to me from…" Rajesh flipped through the papers, "Doctor Gayle, I should be able to find the right combination that works for Maria."

"We've been with Dick for years; he was my doctor when I was a child."

"No offense Henry, but he must be ancient by now. We're not exactly spring chickens ourselves." Rajesh tapped Henry playfully on the shoulder. "I'll be honest, we see this kind of thing all too often from older practitioners. They flick through a medical encyclopaedia, find the drug that best suits the symptoms and prescribe it without checking for interactions. We do have an internal database which can be accessed through a computer, but many of the older surgeries are yet to adapt to the computer generation."

"I had no idea," Henry said.

"Neither did Doctor Gayle by the sounds of it!" Doctor Sharma chuckled. "Don't worry Henry, we'll get Maria sorted. She will have to gradually reduce the intake of her current medication before we make the switch, but she should be a lot better by this time next month."

Henry still looked concerned.

"Honestly, she's safe in my hands."

"I know that, I trust you implicitly, it's just…"

"What is it? Spit it out man."

"The boy Maria was with last night hit his head on our gate. Looked like a right wallop – it knocked him out. I've just checked with the nurse here and apparently he's died."

"What happened?"

"I honestly don't know. The nurse doesn't have any more information. Could you..?"

"Of course, of course. Leave it with me." Doctor Sharma paused. "What are you going to tell Maria?"

Henry sighed. "I have no idea. I don't want her to have another episode – or worse."

Rajesh nodded, deep in thought. "Henry, I understand your concern, but I think you're going to have to be upfront and honest with her. If the boy has died, the police will want to speak with the last person who saw him alive and I presume that would be Maria?"

"Oh my, you're right. Yes, it would be. I hadn't even thought about that."

"Look, if they call, I'll explain that Maria is in no fit state to speak to them right now. I'll find out all I can about this… what was his name?"

"Talik, I don't know his surname. I presume he was around Maria's age as they went to the same school."

Doctor Sharma jotted a few notes down on a blank sheet of paper at the back of his file. "Do you know which ward he was taken to?"

"He went straight into Intensive Care."

"Right." He placed his pen into the inside pocket of his jacket and stood up. "I'll get on this right away and come back when I have more information. You stay with Maria, don't tell her anything just yet and if the police arrive…"

"I'll tell them to bugger off!"

"Exactly!" Doctor Sharma chuckled.

Henry stood up to shake his friend's hand. "I am very glad you're here. Thank you so much for this."

"Don't mention it. I owe you about a thousand times over, this is the least I can do, Captain!" Doctor Sharma smiled as he saluted, walking backwards down the corridor, eventually turning the corner and out of sight. Henry stood motionless for a few moments, listening to the constant drone of medical equipment, muffled voices and telephones ringing. *Elena!* His eyes darted around the hall until he found a sign directing him to the nearest pay-phone. He would have to be very careful with how much information he divulged to his wife.

Elena picked up on the first ring. "Henry! How's Maria doing?"

"She's doing well. She woke up not too long ago and the doctor has checked her over. He says she should be good to come home this evening."

"Oh, that is great news," she replied, her voice shaking. "I've been so worried about her."

"Did you get much sleep?"

"Not really. A couple of hours here and there. Hattie has been her usual amazing self. She woke up with me at 5 and has been keeping me going with endless pots of tea and slices of lemon madeira."

"Maybe you should slow down on the tea, dear, you know how you get after too much caffeine."

"Don't worry, I've switched to rooibos. Thank you for always looking out for me," her smile was audible over the line. "What about that boy Maria was with? How's he doing?"

Henry paused for a moment, unsure of what to say. He hated lying to his wife, but he didn't want to add to her worries. "We're still trying to find out. He was taken to a different ward, but I'll know more later. I'll fill you in when I get back home with Maria."

"It's so wonderful to hear she's doing well. It's been a terrible year for her. I wish there was more we could do to help her. I was thinking, as it's now the summer break, how about we go to the villa in Rennes-le-Château for a week or two? She loves it there. Sunshine, fresh air and relaxation could be just the ticket."

Henry chuckled. "That does sound nice and the wine's not bad either. I'll suggest it to her when she's woken up fully. We could go this weekend." A sudden wave of nausea washed over him as he remembered Talik and the possible police enquiry.

"It will do her the world of good and it would be nice for us to get away as a family. With all the unpleasantness last year, we haven't had a holiday in such a long time. I'll give Nico a call and see if she's around next weekend," Elena announced excitedly.

"Perhaps we should wait until we've spoken with Maria. She may need to rest in bed for a little while longer."

"Right, right, yes, yes. Speak with Maria first and if the doctor gives her the all-clear, we can make plans then," she said, slowing her speech to take another sip of tea. "Did you manage to get any sleep in that chair?"

"Not really. I nodded off a few times, but it was bloody uncomfortable. I'm aching a bit, but I'll survive." He rubbed the back of his neck.

"An early night for us all tonight then."

"Agreed. Right, I'd better get back to Maria."

"Please send her my love."

"I will. See you soon."

Henry hung up the phone, moved out of the little booth and walked back into the corridor. He slowly made his way towards Room 7. As he reached the door, he paused as he gripped the handle and recomposed himself. He ruffled his moustache and forced a broad smile before walking in to see his daughter.

CHAPTER SIX

The police enquiry had been thorough but thankfully brief. The security guard who was on duty at the time, had witnessed Talik hit his head on the gate and fall to the floor. Lord and Lady Braighton's story matched that of the security guard and the paramedics who arrived on the scene minutes later, all gave corroborative accounts – finding Maria unconscious and some distance from the injured boy.

Even though she was not under any suspicion, Maria still held onto the blame. The news of Talik's death had shaken her to the core. She didn't know him well, but she did know he didn't deserve to die. Now back at home, Maria rarely left her room. It was only at her mother's insistence that she came downstairs every day to dine with her parents.

At 6.55pm, Maria pulled on a pair of sweat pants and a baggy T-shirt, ready for her daily attendance around the dinner table. It was Sunday and Hattie had cooked up a hearty roast beef dinner with all the trimmings.

"Here she is," Lord Braighton beamed as he watched his daughter sullenly take her seat at the table. "How are you feeling today sweetheart?"

Maria's subdued smile and passive nod gave

him the answer he wasn't looking for.

"I've asked Doctor Sharma to join us this evening. I know you're finding it difficult to speak to your mother and I, so I thought it might be easier speaking with a professional."

Maria looked up, noticing the doctor for the first time.

"It's good to see you again Maria. I hope you don't mind my being here?"

Maria shook her head. "No, it's fine," she lied. She just wanted to be left alone.

Hattie and the kitchen staff brought in the food. Antique tableware stuffed to the brim with glazed vegetables, roast potatoes, sage and onion stuffing balls, bacon-wrapped sausages, Yorkshire puddings and a huge jug of gravy. The star of the show was the massive rib of beef. As Lord Braighton stood to carve the mighty beast, Maria looked up. "None for me, thank you Daddy."

"You've got to eat to keep your strength up."

"I will eat, I'm just not having any meat. I've decided to be a vegetarian."

Lord Braighton's eyes widened. "But why?"

"I… I just don't want to eat meat anymore," she replied, timidly.

"And you don't have to eat it if you don't want to, does she Henry?" Elena gave her husband 'the look'.

Henry mumbled to himself for a moment, before finding the right words. "But surely that's not good for her, is it Rajesh?"

"Medically speaking, there are plenty of nutrients in other foods, as long as she gets enough protein in her diet from other sources like nuts and eggs." Rajesh shrugged at the Lord. He hated being put on the spot and wanted to back up his friend, but he also wasn't about to lie.

"Hmmm," Henry muttered as he proceeded to slice through the beef, without offering any to his daughter.

Maria spoke very little throughout the meal. She was polite and answered when spoken to, but it was obvious she didn't want to be there. After finishing their meals, Maria asked to be excused. Henry elbowed his friend.

"Actually, would you mind having a little chat first?" Rajesh asked her.

"You can use my office if you'd like," Henry offered.

Now Maria knew this was serious. She was rarely allowed into her father's office and never without him being there.

The last of the day's sun was pouring in through the stained-glass window behind the desk, illuminating the dust particles as they danced in the air. The smell of oiled wood, musty, old books and stale cigar smoke permeated the room. Maria flopped into an old arm chair and stared at her feet as the doctor sat down opposite her.

"How are you feeling, Maria?" Rajesh asked.

"Ok, I guess," Maria replied, noticing her toe nails were in need of a trim. "So, they're worried about me, then?" she asked, deadpanning the doctor.

He smiled momentarily. "Yes, of course, they are. I'm told you've been spending most of your time in your bedroom and not really engaging in conversation."

"What's there to talk about?"

"A lot, I would imagine. There must be a million thoughts running through your head right now. Your parents are feeling a little hopeless at the moment, wanting to help you but not knowing how to. That's why I'm here, to see if there's anything I can do."

Maria swallowed hard and turned away, holding back the tears.

"I imagine this is difficult to articulate, especially to your parents. Situations like this can make us want to hide away from the world and wish the bad thoughts away, but without addressing them, they'll only fester and can be even more damaging to your health and wellbeing. Your parents recognise this and when your father called me, I was only too happy to be a potential sounding board for you. As your doctor, anything you say to me will be kept in the strictest confidence, unless there's anything you want me to tell your parents that you are struggling to verbalise yourself. And if you don't feel comfortable talking to me, that's totally understandable. I can recommend a fantastic therapist who you may feel more of a connection with. Which would you prefer?"

Maria shrugged. "I honestly don't know. I'm

not sure what it is I want. I just can't stop replaying that night in my head. What if I hadn't gone to the dance? What if I had let Charlie drive me and not walked home? What if I hadn't had a panic attack, would Talik would still be alive?" Tears began to fall from her eyes.

"Maria, you mustn't think like that," he said gently. "What happened was a tragic accident and no part of the blame falls on you." Rajesh's heart went out to the young girl. "We can't change the past, no matter how much we wish it, but we can learn how to accept it."

Maria's breath began to shake as she fought against her emotions. Rajesh looked around until he found a box of tissues and handed them to her. She nodded in thanks and wiped her face.

"How do I move on from this?"

"This is a good first step. Opening up and talking about what happened will help you come to terms with it. The new medication I prescribed should also help and we'll keep reviewing that until we have the right balance. Have you had any more panic attacks since starting it?"

Maria shook her head. "No, thankfully. I thought I was going to have one last night when I couldn't sleep, but I managed to stop it."

"That's great news. It will take a few weeks for them to fully get into your system, but I'm pleased you're already seeing the results."

"I think the medication might be keeping me awake though. I'm really tired, all the time, but I only managed a few hours a night."

"Are you spending most of your time in bed?"

Maria nodded.

"It could be that you're not getting enough exercise and therefore your body isn't tired enough to sleep."

"Are you sure you're not just saying that to get me out of my bedroom?" Maria said, smiling for the first time.

The doctor chuckled. "No and yes. Of course, you shouldn't be shutting yourself away from the world but I'm also serious about the need for exercise. Especially as you're a vegetarian now."

"Did you see the look on my Dad's face when I told him□"

"Yes, I thought his eyes were going to pop out of his head." The doctor chuckled. "It's not the first time I've seen your father in that state, but it's definitely the first time I've seen him able to rein in his emotions."

"He must be worried about me. I expected him to go crazy. I knew he wouldn't be happy about it, but it's something I need to do."

"Why do you say that?"

Maria's smiled faded. "Killing innocent animals, blood, death – I don't want any part of it."

The doctor nodded. "Ah, I understand, completely. After what you've been through, that's a perfectly reasonable reaction. And don't worry about Henry, I'll smooth things over with him. I can't guarantee he'll be happy about it, but once I've explained,

I'm sure he'll get used to the idea. As long as I have your permission to tell him."

Maria nodded. "Please do. I feel a lot safer with it coming from you rather than me."

They both chuckled.

"It's good to hear you laugh."

"It's the first time I have, since…" she trailed off before smiling at the doctor. "Thank you."

"You're very welcome."

"You were right, it has felt good to talk about this."

"Great! And you shouldn't stop here. How do you feel about talking to the therapist I mentioned?"

Maria nodded. "Yeah, I think that might be a good idea."

"Excellent, I'll make the call tomorrow."

"Thanks."

"And what about your parents?"

Maria frowned. "Do you want me to tell them what I've told you?"

"No, not necessarily, but I'm sure they'd like to know how you're doing."

Maria thought for a moment before answering. "As you're already telling my Dad about me being a vegetarian, could you also tell them about everything we've discussed? It's just so difficult opening up to them; if that's ok?"

"Of course, it is. I'm sure it will go some way to alleviate their worries. Oh, and one more thing before you leave."

Maria raised an eyebrow.

"Your mother would like to book a trip to France. You don't have to give an answer right away, but would you at least consider it please?"

Flashes of happier times shared with her family at their villa in the south of France flooded her mind. She nodded.

"Great, I'm sure your parents will be glad to hear that and personally, I believe it would do you the world of good to get away." He stood up with her. "Maria, what happened was an accident, completely out of your control. I know you can't believe it right now, but these feelings will ease over time. There's no sense in torturing yourself. If you want your doctor's advice, you should go to France, spend time away from the manor and try to relax. And if you ever need to chat, my door is always open."

"Thanks." Maria grabbed the door knob but turned back to the doctor before leaving. "Could you tell Mum and Dad I'm going for a bath please? I don't really want to be in the room when you tell them everything."

"Not a problem," the doctor smiled.

As Maria walked back to her bedroom, she felt a sense of relief, like a huge weight had been lifted from her. The wall of pain she had built up around her was finally beginning to crack and crumble away. It would take time to heal, but her talk with the doctor had really put things into perspective. This was the beginning of her recovery and now, all she wanted, was to have a long soak in the tub to clear her head.

Downstairs, Rajesh walked into the sitting room where Elena and Henry were patiently waiting.

"How did it go?" Henry asked abruptly, before the doctor had even had chance to sit down.

"It went well." Rajesh said, taking his seat. "Really well, actually."

Elena sighed in relief. "How is she?"

"Grieving, blaming herself for the accident, unable to control her negative thoughts."

"How is any of that, good?" Henry asked, pouring his friend a brandy.

"Henry, hush!" Elena scolded.

"She's young and confused but she's also incredibly intelligent and after our little talk, I believe she will start to improve."

"What did you say?"

"Not a lot really, I just gave her a little advice and reinforced what she already knew, deep down." He turned to Elena. "She's considering your proposal to go to France. I wouldn't pressure her on the subject, but I'd be surprised if she doesn't decide to go. Some time away from the manor is exactly what the doctor orders." He chuckled at his little pun, before taking a sip of brandy. "Oh, and Henry, the vegetarian thing seems to be a phase. The vision of seeing that boy laid out, with blood pouring from his head is haunting her. I believe that's the reason she doesn't want to eat meat, but once she's feeling better, there's a good chance she'll drop the whole vegetarian thing."

"Ah, that makes sense. It would never have occurred to me that… That poor boy. Tragic. It's been so difficult knowing how to speak to Maria after everything that has happened. Thank you for coming over tonight."

"Any time, my old friend."

Maria slowly sank into the warm, bubbling water. She felt her body relax and the tension release in her muscles. The scented bubble bath warmed her nose as she inhaled, breathing deeply and peacefully. With the taps still running, she submerged her head under the water and closed her eyes, allowing the muffled sounds to ease her troubled mind. The warm water suspended her and with weightlessness came a sense of freedom; a brief, but welcome, respite from the grip of anxiety.

Suddenly, a sharp pain in her stomach made her open her eyes and bolt up, out of the water. Her eyes stung from the soap and she instinctively closed them while clumsily reaching for a towel. As she wiped her face, a distinct laughter echoed throughout the steamy bathroom. Maria froze. She recognised that sound. Slowly removing the towel from her face and adjusting her vision through the thick fog, she turned her head towards the laughter. There, sitting on the toilet seat, swinging his legs, was Mr Piggy. He giggled maniacally; his eyes boring into hers. Unable to speak, Maria stared back, her mouth wide open. Mr Piggy stopped laughing and jumped down from the toilet. He cocked his head to one side and pouted, looking quizzically at her, as if seeing her for the first time. He slowly moved across the room; his gaze fixed on the startled girl in the bath. When he was by her side, he paused. Neither of them moved. Suddenly, he slapped her across the head and began screaming, "filthy bitch, filthy bitch, filthy bitch!" He taunted her, dancing around the bathroom, shouting and laughing. Maria scrambled to get up, out of the tub, water cascading over the sides. She spun around to face him, but Mr Piggy was gone. She was all alone.

CHAPTER SEVEN

Lord and Lady Braighton sipped their cocktails as Maria stared out of the window of the private jet. She loved flying. Soaring through the clouds, seeing the boats sail across the ocean and watching the small houses come into view as they made their descent. She only wished the flight had been longer. After landing at a small airport in Carcassonne, the Braightons were met by a smartly dressed chauffeur, Jean-Henri. He stood at the bottom of the metal boarding stairs, straightening his cap and brushing down his uniform with his gloved hands. When the door to the jet opened, he applied his practiced smile as he watched Lord Braighton disembark.

It was another hour by car to get to their villa in Rennes-le-Château, but Maria always enjoyed the drive. The anticipation of almost being on holiday and spending long, summer days in the quintessential French countryside. As the car weaved through the narrow country roads, Maria watched the farms and villages whizz by as she rested her head on her arms against the open window ledge. Occasionally, she would snap blurry pictures of the wildlife or wave at nonchalant sheep, standing idly in the fields. The idyllic scenery was the perfect tonic to soothe her mind after the recent, tragic events.

The car slowed as they turned off the main road and into a remote village.

"Look at all these tourists," Lady Braighton exclaimed as she peered out of the window. Groups of people were milling around outside, looking at maps, pointing towards buildings and taking very little notice of the traffic behind them. "That bloody BBC documentary. I'd hoped people would have forgotten about it by now, it's been a couple of years since it was broadcast."

Lord Braighton looked up from his newspaper and regarded the people outside. "Bloody vultures. A sniff of treasure and they're all out in force."

"I think it's nice," Maria interjected. "I like seeing people in the village."

"Your grandfather would be furious. He built the property here after the war because it wasn't a tourist hotspot. After serving his country, he deserved his solitude, surrounded by beauty. He would have hated all of these people bothering him."

"That wasn't the only reason he chose this area dear," Lady Braighton smiled knowingly at her husband.

"Humph." The Lord pulled his paper back up, shielding his face.

"Oh, you mean Grandad's lady friend?" Maria said, innocently.

"Enough!" Lord Braighton huffed. "I don't want this discussed in my presence. What my father did after my mother's death was his business and his alone."

Lady Braighton nodded to her daughter, rolling her eyes, which made them both titter. Lord Braighton peered from over his newspaper and shot them both a stern look, prompting more laughter.

The car slowed to a halt.

"What's the problem Jean-Henri?" Lord Braighton asked the driver.

"There is a line of cars trying to turn into le stationnement, but not so many exiting."

"Can't you stop by the side of the road? We only need to pop into the shop," Lady Braighton asked through the partition.

"Pop?"

"We just need milk and bread," Lord Braighton boomed.

"Ah, oui. No madame, pardon, but there is not enough room for the vehicle."

"Damn it. That documentary has a lot to answer for." She spun around and folded her arms in a temper.

Maria was still staring out the window, watching the tourists. *Who are these people? How far have they travelled? Where are they staying?* She turned around to face her parents. "My English teacher was really excited when I told him we holidayed here. Apparently, he went to university with Henry Lincoln, the man who created the documentary series and who's now writing a book about the Holy Grail's link to Rennes-le-Château."

"Great, that's all we need. More fuel on the tourist bonfire. If it gets any worse, we'll have to sell up and find another quiet corner of the world." Lady Braighton was not amused.

Henry folded up his newspaper and placed it by his side. "I don't think it will come to that Elena. Television is one thing, but I doubt a book could ever have that kind of impact. Not in this day and age. It's all stuff and nonsense anyway. Grail legends have been circulating for centuries. People look, they find nothing and give up, until a newer generation picks up the mantle and the cycle continues anew. Everyone loves a mystery and there are very few more mysterious than the Knights Templar. The Holy Grail and the bloodline of Christ? Poppycock! Let this charlatan release his book, I doubt it will lead to any more tourists. Mark my words, it will die down soon enough. I don't even know why we come into the village anyway – the villa is self-sufficient."

"We need daily essentials like milk, bread and eggs."

"The staff have known for a week we were coming. I'm sure the pantry is fully stocked; what else could we need?"

Lady Braighton ignored her husband and turned to Maria. "Do you mind hopping out of the car and popping into the shop for me, please dear? Nico said she would make up a hamper for us, as long as those tourists haven't got their grubby paws on its contents first."

Maria nodded and opened the car door. The midday sun was bright and warmed her pale skin as she made her way past groups of people speaking in many different languages. She loved being around them and would have liked to stop and chat, but her parents were already in a mood from staying in the car this long, any longer and they'd be unbearable. She quickened her pace to the shop. The streets were crowded and as she neared Nico's delicatessen, there was a line of people stretching outside, waiting to be served. She joined the back of the queue and peered through the large, shop window at the rows of delectable cakes, pastries and baguettes. Salivating at the tempting offerings, Maria was momentarily distracted from her surrounds until a young Japanese woman tapped her shoulder and pointed into the shop. Nico was standing behind the counter waving at her, beckoning her inside. Grumbles and dramatic sighs were sounded by the patrons she squeezed past to gain entry. Nico was waiting inside with a huge smile and her arms wide open. She whisked her up into a friendly hug and kissed both cheeks, much to the chagrin of the waiting customers.

"Oh, it's so good to see you, ma chérie."

"You too Nico. Busy today I see!"

"Yes, very. Michel is here also, but he is on his break, so I can't chat for long, I'm afraid. I'll come over this evening and we talk then."

"Sounds great!"

Nico walked to the back of the shop and carried out a huge hamper stuffed full with goodies. "Where's the car?"

"Just around the corner, it couldn't get down the street."

"Will you be ok carrying this?"

Maria took hold of the basket. It was heavy, perhaps a little too heavy, but the car wasn't too far away. "I'll be fine," she groaned, lifting it up.

Nico scrunched up her face. "Hmmm, non, this won't do." She reached into the basket and pulled out two bottles of wine. "This will make it lighter. Please tell your mother, I shall bring over the rest tonight. She may worry when she notices the alcohol is missing," Nico chuckled.

"I don't know why she's ordered wine; we have lots in the cellar."

"Ah, but this is Beaujolais Nouveau, a special wine only produced once a year in very small amounts. I have been saving these bottles for your mother for months." As Nico spoke, she placed the bottles behind her and reached into the hamper. She pulled together the overhanging sides of the red and white cloth which lined the basket and tied it in the middle, securing the contents inside. "There, now everything is safe."

The customers started murmuring.

"Pardon, I must get back to work." She kissed Maria's cheeks. "Jusqu'à ce soir."

It was difficult navigating out of the small shop and through the narrow streets with the large, wicker basket, but Maria kept a tight grip on the handle of the hamper and was soon back at the car.

"My goodness, what did you order?" Lord Braighton stared at the huge basket Maria was sliding onto the seat before climbing in herself.

"Just a few essentials," Elena informed him, without meeting his gaze.

"Essentials?" Lord Braighton asked incredulously.

"Yes darling. You know, things for us to eat and drink." She opened the chequered cloth and picked up a loaf of bread. "Things we need in order to survive."

Henry reached into the basket and pulled out a jar of foie gras. "We need this to survive, do we?"

Elena chidingly tapped his hand and retrieved the pâté, placing it back inside the basket.

"Are we all ready to go?" the driver asked.

"Yes, we are, thank you Jean-Henri."

As the car slowly navigated through the tourists, Lady Braighton rummaged to the bottom of hamper.

"If you're looking for wine, Nico had to take it out so that the basket would be easier for me to carry."

"Oh!" Lady Braighton remarked, dejectedly.

"Don't worry Mum, she said she would bring it over tonight after she's closed the shop."

"I'm sure I can wait until then." Lady Braighton smiled, inspecting the contents more closely. She sniffed the fresh bread and inspected the cheeses. "Such wonderful food. I can't wait to see what she brings over tonight with the rest of it."

"Rest?" Lord Braighton's eyebrows were in fear of hitting the roof of the car.

Elena ignored her husband, instead turning

back to Maria. "Thank you for picking this up, darling. How was Nico?"

"Frantic! Her shop is crammed full of people today."

"I'm not surprised. It's the only shop for miles around. It was manageable before when it was only serving locals and the occasional passing trade, but now it's just gotten silly with all of these tourists. I hope she's not too overwhelmed."

"Actually, I think she likes it. She was rushed off her feet, but still smiling."

"Nico is always smiling. It's one of the reasons why we bonded so quickly. I suppose the extra income can't be a bad thing either."

The car pulled out of the village and into the mountains. The roads were narrower here with barely enough room for two passing cars. Fertiliser had recently been spread across the fields and Lord Braighton asked Maria to wind up the window to keep out the smell. She didn't mind so much; she could still watch the scenery through the glass. As the trees receded, they gave way to the open countryside. Maria could see for miles around her – grasslands, farm buildings and mountains in the distance. The rivers mostly flowed underground, but every once in a while, a stream would present itself. As the car slowed to give way to a tractor, Maria spotted an isolated, small pool of water. She watched the birds diving for insects, cattle quenching their thirst and the reflections on the surface as it rippled and waved, glistening in the afternoon sun. Two sheep nudged each other out of the way to get to the best spot, which made Maria giggle. It was then she saw something. She leaned closer to the window, pressing her face against the glass to get a clearer view. There was something or someone in the centre of the pool, she was sure of it. It bobbed on the surface for a moment, before diving into the water. She thought she saw a face, but wasn't sure. Its head popped up again, only for a moment, making Maria recoil into her seat. That was Mr Piggy. A cold shiver ran through Maria's body and her pulse began to race. *Was that really him?* As the tractor pulled away onto a side lane, the car regained its momentum, moving them away. *This was ridiculous. How could Mr Piggy be here?* She needed to make sure. Climbing up on her seat, she stared out of the back window, but the view of the pool was gone, hidden behind mounds of grasslands. Relaxing back into her seat, she told herself that it was just her imagination playing tricks on her.

After a few more miles, the villa came into view. It sat majestically, perched on the edge of the hillside, with stunning, panoramic views of the surrounding countryside. The late Lord Braighton – Henry's father – had chosen this particular spot after his extensive travels through the region. He selected somewhere remote, a place where he could relax and escape the grind of everyday life. That desire for seclusion had resonated throughout the family. As the car pulled into the drive, a wave of calm swept over the Braightons. This was exactly what they needed right now. Two weeks away from their problems and hopefully, a healing experience for Maria.

The staff were already inside, preparing lunch for the family. Jean-Henri brought in the luggage and after a shower and change of clothes, the family sat outside on the large veranda. The afternoon heat was radiating off the foliage, but shaded underneath their canopy, sipping ice-cold, freshly-squeezed lemonade with fruit picked from their orchard, the Braightons felt at peace.

"I've missed this place," Lady Braighton breathed, finishing her glass of lemonade and pouring another from the ice-filled jug on the table beside her.

"I'd almost forgotten how beautiful it is here," added Maria, watching the insects pollinating the flowers around the edge of the balcony.

Lord Braighton smiled at his daughter. He wasn't an overly emotional man, but seeing Maria happy for the first time in a long time, warmed his heart. The new medication Doctor Sharma had prescribed seemed to be working wonders.

"Are you ready for lunch, sir?"

"Yes, thank you Julio. We'll eat out here if that's alright?"

"Certainly sir."

The old butler walked away and signalled the staff to bring out the food; stacking trays filled with delicacies from both French and Spanish cuisines. Being so close to Spain, Rennes-le-Château had an amalgamation of cultures influenced from natives of both countries, co-existing in and around the border.

"This looks fantastic, a real feast for the eyes," Lady Braighton marvelled at the dishes being brought in.

"I told you we didn't need anything from the shop."

"Oh Henry! Nico is a friend – I will always want to support her. Besides, she bakes the finest bread. These sandwiches have been made with the loaf we just picked up."

Maria selected one of the sandwich bites and bit into the serrano ham and sun-dried tomato filling. "This is delicious!"

Elena pointed to her daughter. "You see, Maria loves it."

"Hmmm, I'll be the judge, thank you very much." Henry selected a ham and cheese sandwich, biting into the crisp, dark-coloured baguette. "OK, I agree, that is bloody good bread."

Through joyous exchanges, the family ate their way through the wide selection of delicious food. With full bellies, plenty of refreshing drinks and light-hearted conversation, the hours soon slipped away until eventually, the sun began its descent beneath the mountains, casting deep, red and orange streaks across the dusk sky.

"It's getting a little chilly," Lady Braighton announced. "I might go inside for a while and wait until Nico arrives. Will you be staying out here?"

"For a little longer," Lord Braighton indicated he was only half way through smoking his cigar.

"What about you Maria?"

"I'll stay out here with Dad if that's alright?"

"Of course. Let me know if you need me to bring your cardigan out."

Elena closed the patio door behind her, leaving her husband and daughter alone. For a while no one spoke. Their seats were facing the view ahead of them and both were taken in by the magnificent sunset. It was Lord Braighton who broke the silence.

"How are you feeling now, Maria?"

"I'm fine, thanks Dad, I don't feel the cold as quickly as Mum."

"That's not what I meant."

"I know," Maria smiled. "I'm getting there. Being here definitely helps."

"Good, I'm pleased to hear it." He took a puff of his cigar. "I understand it's difficult opening up to your mother and I, but there really is nothing you can't tell us. We may be old and a little out of touch with modern society, but you are our daughter and we love you. You can come to us with anything and we will always be there for you."

"Thank you, Daddy. I do know that. It doesn't make it any easier to talk about though, especially as I don't fully understand what I'm feeling."

"How's the new medication?"

"A few side-effects, but nothing major. Doctor Sharma said it would take a few weeks to start working fully, although I'm already feeling the benefits. I still feel sad sometimes, but it's not as overwhelming anymore. Last week it was debilitating."

Henry nodded, knowing how scary it was for him and Elena to see their daughter in such bad shape. "Just take each day as it comes. Time is a great healer and there are few places in the world more relaxing than here."

"That's the truth." Maria clinked her glass with her father's and they finished their drinks.

Henry put out his cigar and rose from his seat. "Come on young lady, let's not leave your mother all on her own. I'm sure she'll want to play cards or," Henry shuddered theatrically, "Monopoly!"

"It wouldn't be a holiday without you losing all your money, staying at all my hotels. Sounds like the perfect evening to me," she laughed.

"One day I might surprise you and win at that game. Are you coming?"

"I'll be in in a moment; I just want to watch the sunset for a little longer."

"OK darling, take as much time as you need."

Maria turned back to the view and watched the last of the days light slowly disappear. As a flock of birds swept across the sky, a quiet calm descended on the landscape. She felt at peace.

CHAPTER EIGHT

With a bumpy landing came the crash back to reality Maria had been dreading. Those serene two weeks at the villa had flown by and as the jet taxied into Arrivals, it already felt like a distant memory. The car journey home was eerily silent, with everyone able to feel the building tension as they neared Braighton Manor. The blood on the grass outside had been cleaned away weeks ago, but the images of that night were burned into their collective minds, forever. Maria turned away from the window and closed her eyes, desperately wishing she could have stayed at the villa. As the gates slowly swung open, she began to shiver involuntarily. Her father's arm was immediately around her, pulling her close to him. With her head buried into his chest, she hugged him back, grateful for his support.

For the next few days, Maria stayed inside the house. She closed the curtains in her bedroom, shutting out the summer weather and sat at her desk for long intervals, excusing herself with having homework to finish. When every essay was written and every book read, she was still reluctant to leave the house. On the final weekend before the start of the new school year, Maria lay in bed, staring at the beam of light pouring in through a crack in the curtains. She watched it slowly move across the ceiling, as if it were her own, personal sundial.

The bedroom door suddenly opened and Lady Braighton stomped through the gloom and over to the window, pulling back the drapes and flooding the room in glorious light. Maria groaned and dove back underneath the covers.

"Maria Anne Braighton!" she scolded. "What are you doing, still in bed? It's almost noon." Without waiting for a reply, Elena opened up the wardrobe and selected a few items of clothing.

"Mum, what are you doing?"

"Oh! She is awake then!" Elena's sarcasm dripped from her lips as she continued to sort through Maria's clothes. "We're going out dear. I've made reservations for lunch at The Ivy."

"In London?"

"There's only one Ivy dear."

"I… I don't… erm."

Lady Braighton turned around, softer now. "I know this is difficult and we've left you alone for the past few weeks, hoping it would help, but I fear it's done the opposite. You're going back to school in three days and if we don't get you out of this room now, I fear you'll never leave."

"But Mum…"

"Go and have a shower, I've laid your clothes out over there and Charlie will be waiting to drive us in half an hour. That's 30 minutes, Maria. Whatever state of dress you're in at that point is how you'll be presented in London, so I suggest you get ready." Elena walked over to her stunned daughter and kissed the top of her head. "I love you," she whispered, before leaving the room.

Maria was still in a state of shock when the door closed behind Elena. *Where did that come from?* she thought. Glancing over at the clock on her bedside table, she saw it was almost 12. Knowing her mother, she would be true to her word and the last thing Maria wanted was to be shoddily dressed in one of London's premier restaurants. The Ivy was a hot-spot for celebrities. What if she bumped into Harrison Ford, Mark Hamill and Carrie Fisher having a spot of lunch between filming? She was sure she'd seen their pictures in the paper as they exited the restaurant only a few months ago, when they were promoting 'The Empire Strikes Back'.

Bouncing out of bed, she tied up her hair and stumbled over to the bathroom to brush her teeth and dive into the shower. With exactly one minute remaining, Maria walked down the stairs where her mother and Charlie were already waiting for her. Elena was comically tapping her watch.

"I just need to put my shoes on and I'll be ready."

"And maybe run a brush through your hair in the car?"

"Oh!" Maria's hands touched the top of her head and released her still tied-up hair. "I knew I didn't have enough time to dry it, so decided not to get it wet in the shower."

"Good thinking." Elena smiled. "There's a

brush in the living room, in the drawer, next to the chaise lounge. We'll be waiting over by the car."

Maria felt a jolt of excitement. She loved The Ivy and the thrill of spending the afternoon in London with her mother was always cause for celebration. In the living room, she walked over to the chaise lounge and quickly found the brush tucked away in the side table drawer. She placed it by her side as she sat down to put on her shoes. She was smiling as she slipped on the heels. The butterflies in her stomach rose through her body and caused her eyes to water with joy. She sighed happily and picked up the other shoe, noticing something on the side of it. *Was that a scratch?* Bringing it up to her eyes, she peered more closely at the dark smudge.

A scream from inside the house made Lady Braighton turn sharply around from the car and dash back into the manor. Maria was curled up in the foetal position on the chaise lounge, rocking and sobbing. One of her shoes had been thrown to the other side of the room.

"What happened? Are you alright?"

For a moment, Maria could only babble, losing her ability to form words. Lady Braighton hugged and comforted her until she was able to speak. "Blood. There's blood on my shoe."

When Henry arrived home and found his wife holding his wailing daughter, he'd called Doctor Sharma, who had made his way over to the manor.

"I've given her a sedative to help her sleep tonight and upped the dose of her medication. I really think she needs to see the therapist I recommended. There is only so much medication can do. He's not cheap, but he's the best in the country. If anyone is able to help Maria, it's him."

"Set it up please Rajesh and don't worry about the cost. Maria's well-being is far more important."

"I've already spoken with him, so he knows the details, but I'll call him again in the morning and see when he's next available."

"Will she have to go to London to see him?" Elena asked. "I don't know how easy it will be to get Maria to leave the house, especially after today."

"I'm sure he can make an exception."

"She's meant to be going back to school on Tuesday. Do you think she should?"

"I'll be honest, Elena, I don't think so and I wouldn't push her to go back either. She's trauma-tised and incredibly delicate right now. I think you should look at getting her home-schooled for the foreseeable future. Going back to school, with every-one asking her questions about that night... it could be too much for her."

Elena gripped her husband's hand.

"She will be alright; it may just take a little more time."

"I checked the shoes myself, there was no blood on them," Lady Braighton said, lowering her voice. "She's not going mad, is she? Seeing things that aren't there?"

"It may have been she remembered those were

the shoes she'd worn at the dance and mistaken a smudge or a shadow as the boy's blood. She's a bright girl, she's just not emotionally mature enough to be able to deal with this amount of trauma so early in her life."

"I don't think anyone's really ready, at any age. My poor girl."

"She'll be alright dear. Rajesh is the best doctor I know and as long as we facilitate a comfortable environment for her, she'll be back to her old self in no time."

"She's lucky to have you both as parents." Rajesh stood up to leave. "If you need me, no matter the time, just give me a call and I'll be here as soon as I can."

"Thank you so much."

"You're a good man Rajesh." Lord Braighton stood to shake his friend's hand.

"The next few months might be a bit rocky, but with therapy, the right balance of medication and people she knows and loves around her, in time, this will all seem like a distant memory."

CHAPTER NINE

"Daddy, I'll be fine."

Maria was standing in the hallway of Braighton Manor, suitcases by her side.

"But you're only twenty-two Maria. Why do you have to move out so soon? I don't like the idea of you being alone."

"I won't be alone, Daddy. Hattie will be with me, so you don't have to worry about me not feeding myself properly."

"And Charlie will be available if you ever need a driver," Lady Braighton interjected.

Lord Braighton gave his wife a stern look.

"Oh Henry, we knew this day was coming. You have to acknowledge that our little girl is not so little anymore. She's a woman now and doesn't want to live her whole life in our shadows."

Lord Braighton sighed. He wasn't happy to see his daughter leave the nest, but he knew his wife was right.

"I'll only be in London, Daddy. I'm sure I'll be visiting here often."

"Too bloody right you will. You may be all grown up, but you are still my little princess."

Maria hugged her parents as her father uncharacteristically let out a small tear, careful to wipe it away before anyone noticed.

Lord Braighton straightened himself and looked seriously at his daughter. "If you ever need us, your mother and I will always be here for you. Remember that."

"I will Daddy, thank you." Maria kissed her parents and walked to the front door where the butler was waiting to open it. He smiled at her and bowed his head slightly, as she made her way outside and down the steps to the waiting town car. She watched as Hattie placed the last of the bags inside the boot of the large vehicle. It was a fresh, spring morning and as Maria inhaled, she could smell the azaleas. A thousand memories rushed into her head.

I'm really leaving, Maria thought as she stood motionless by the side of the Rolls Royce. *This is no longer my home.*

"Here ya' go miss," the driver smiled as he opened the car door.

Snapping out of her fleeting, dream-like state, she smiled back at him. "Thank you, Charlie."

Maria slowly climbed into the car, placing her Gucci clutch in the recess between the two expansive seats. Charlie had provided her with a cold bottle of water which sat in the cup holder, next to a box of tissues. As the door closed behind her, Maria relaxed, enjoying the feel of the cool leather on her warm body. Charlie and Hattie moved to the back of the car. Knowing she couldn't be seen behind the tinted glass, she closed her eyes and breathed deeply as tears silently flowed down her face. Allowing the flood of emotions to wash over her, she remembered growing up, playing in the gardens, finding hidden areas of the house to explore and spending long, glorious days playing board games with her family. Helping to build a tree house with the gardeners, away from the disproving eyes of her father, baking in the kitchen with Hattie and hosting grand events with her parents. A lifetime of memories; but not all were happy. Doctors, pain, confusion, her imaginary friend, Talik… A light tapping on the window pulled her back to the present. Maria grabbed a handful of tissues and quickly dried her face, so that Hattie wouldn't see the tears. Pressing the button by her side, she rolled down the window.

"Your parents are waving at you Miss," Hattie said, pointing back towards to the house.

Maria beamed a perfect smile, waving and blowing kisses to her parents, who were standing on the steps of Braighton Manor.

"They're going to miss you," Hattie whispered through the open window before walking to the front of the car.

"And I shall miss them," Maria replied quietly to herself, while still maintaining a smile for her parents.

"Ready to go?" Charlie asked cheerfully through the car's intercom system. Maria pressed a button above her head, "Yes, thank you, I'm ready."

As they pulled away, she stuck her arm out of the window and frantically waved to her parents, holding as broad a smile as she could muster. Once the car had turned away from the house and was heading down the long, Cypress tree-lined private road, Maria rolled up the window and let her face fall. Hidden behind tinted windows and a partition from the front of the car, she allowed herself to cry again, except this time, she didn't stop the tears.

The past few years had been a worrying time, for everyone. Maria had declined to return to school, even when the medication and therapy was working to curb her 'adolescent episodes', as one therapist had called them. Her home-schooling had provided a good education and at one point, she had contemplated university, but thoughts of the past would hinder her future prospects. That was until her twenty-second birthday. Her life was one of privilege. She had loving, doting parents and never wanted for anything – anything except a life beyond these walls. The last time she had tried independence, it had ending in disaster – but that was years ago. She was an adult now and things had changed; she had changed. For months she contemplated what she really wanted to do and reasoned, if she didn't gain her independence soon, she could very easily spend the rest of her life living in the manor. It took some convincing before her parents accepted this abrupt change in attitude, but eventually, they both agreed that it was Maria's decision to make. Lord Braighton bought a flat for her in Kensington. She had protested, but he had insisted, explaining that not only would it put his mind at ease, a Central London property would only ever increase in value, therefore this was as much an investment for him as it was a home for her. She of course knew that was his way of ending the argument. He had never shown any interest in property before.

Thanks to Doctor Sharma, Maria hadn't had an 'episode' in over two years and had slowly been reducing the amount of medication she took. Through therapy, she had accepted that the events of the worst night of her life, were not her fault. She'd even mustered up the courage to visit Talik's grave on more than one occasion. It was difficult at first, but she needed to pay her respects and try to close that chapter of her life. Time, as everyone told her, had indeed been a great healer. Now, no longer dependant on psychotropic drugs, she felt the fog lift from her mind and was able to deal with her thoughts and memories in a more controlled way. She still took antidepressants, but only a low dose to keep her serotonin levels in check. For the first time in her life, she felt strong enough to stand up on her own and explore the world outside the confines of Braighton Manor.

Traffic was heavy on the roads from Kent to London, giving Maria enough time to pull herself together and look forward to a future she was in control of. By the time the car pulled up to her new home, she was excited for whatever adventures lay ahead of her.

The first few weeks were thrilling for Maria. A stream of people were constantly flowing through her little maisonette in Kensington, helping with the unpacking and dressing of the exquisite garden flat – with Hattie's guidance.

Hattie had worked for the family for over 30 years and was like as a second mother to Maria. This was uncharted territory for the young Braighton and knowing that a friendly face was mere meters away from her at any given moment, was a great comfort.

The following Sunday, instead of going back to the manor, Maria invited her parents to her new home.

"I love what you've done with the place darling," Lady Braighton commented cheerfully as soon as she walked through the front door.

"Hmmm. It's a little small," remarked Lord Braighton.

"Henry!" Elena gave her husband 'the look', which made Maria smile.

"It may not be the grand home you're used to, but it's big enough for me. The three bedrooms are of a good size and the small annex off the back, is perfect for Hattie. She's very comfortable in there."

Maria walked her parents into the drawing room where Hattie was pouring tea. The three Braightons sat around the large, circular coffee table in front of the fireplace as they were served afternoon refreshments.

"Is this the china your grandmother gave you?" Lady Braighton asked, admiring her tea cup.

"It is Mummy. Don't worry, I only intend on using it for special occasions."

"Oh no dear. Your grandmother loved this tea set, but she always said that crockery was meant to be used, not hidden away in a cupboard. She would want you to get as much use out of it as possible."

Maria smiled and placed her hand onto her mother's. Henry was slowly sipping his tea whilst looking around the room, taking in his surroundings. He placed his cup back into the saucer, ruffled his moustache and looked at his daughter.

"Are you happy here, Maria?"

"So far, so good Daddy. To be honest, I haven't had any time to myself yet. What with the removal company, builders and decorators, the past few weeks have been pretty frantic. It has been nice to put my own stamp on the place, though. I loved living with you and Mum, but it's also good to have a place I can call my own."

Lord Braighton nodded slowly and took another sip of tea.

Hattie walked into the room and announced that lunch was ready. The Braightons moved to the adjoining dining room where a feast of food was spread out on the large table. Eager to impress her parents and put her father's doubts to rest, Maria had hired a chef for the day, to help Hattie cater their meal.

"This all looks wonderful darling," Lady Braighton said as she sat down to the table.

With a glint in his eye, Henry admired the centrepiece "Is that suckling roast pig?"

"It is, Daddy. I know it's your favourite."

"I thought we'd be eating some vegetarian dish."

"As long as I don't have to prepare or eat it, I don't mind serving you what you like. You accepted me as a vegetarian in your home, so I can accept you as a meat-eater in mine."

The old man's face lit up as Hattie sliced the pork and served it to Lord and Lady Braighton. Maria was pleased to have made her father smile. With plenty of food and wine, the good spirits continued throughout the afternoon and into the evening.

Once her parents left and Hattie had retired to the annex, Maria found herself alone for the first time since moving in. She walked over to the shelf and selected a book, taking it with her to a large, comfy chair by the open fireplace. Outside, she could hear the muffled sound of traffic moving on the roads, but inside, it was eerily silent. A nervous feeling came over her, one she hadn't felt in some time. She shook it off and forced a smile. *I need to get used to this,* she thought. *You're a grown woman now Maria, this will be good for you.* She settled in by the fire and began to read the book.

That night, Maria found it difficult to sleep. The quiet of her home made her nervous and a mild panic had risen in her chest. The more she tried to brush it off, the stronger the feeling of dread. The next morning, as the sunlight illuminated her curtains, Maria lay there with tears in her eyes, frustrated with herself. She'd been awake most of the night and was now staring up at the ceiling, just as she had as a child. *Why can't I just be 'normal'?* Suddenly an ear-piercing scream jolted Maria upright. She jumped out of bed, and followed the panicked sounds down the stairs, until she was standing outside the door to the annex. The screaming was coming from inside. She banged heavily on the locked door and rattled the handle.

"Hattie, let me in! What's happening in there? Are you OK?"

The screaming became gargled as if someone was being choked and then suddenly, it stopped. Maria put her ear to the door, but could no longer hear anything.

"Hattie! Hattie! Please, open the door."

There was no response.

Worried her maid was seriously injured, Maria ran into the kitchen and retrieved the spare key to the room. She shakily unlocked the door but was met by an unknown force, blocking her entry.

"Hattie. It's just me. Please let me in."

Maria leaned on the door and pushed with all of her might. It unexpectedly gave way and she fell into the room, landing hard onto the wooden floor and bruising her arm. As she cradled her elbow, she heard a muffled giggle.

"Who's there?"

The giggling stopped.

Using the door handle as a grip, Maria pulled herself up and switched on the light. Hattie was laying naked on top of the bed, sheets strewn all over the floor, some of which had gathered behind the door and was presumably the cause of her clumsy entrance. Maria rushed over to Hattie. Dark, red marks were scratched all over her chest, which looked as if someone had been clawing at her.

"Hattie. Are you ok? What happened?"

With urgency, Maria checked her pulse. There was one, but it was very faint.

"I'm going to call an ambulance. I'll be right back."

As she turned to walk out of the room, she slipped on one of the sheets and fell onto the bed, landing on Hattie's legs. The giggling returned.

In shock and fear, Maria's eyes darted around the room, expecting to see someone else there with them, but there wasn't. Had she tripped or was she pushed? She cautiously moved off the bed and carefully made her way out of the annex; her eyes inspecting every corner of the kitchen - except for the floor. Something touched her foot. Maria screamed and kicked her legs forward; jumping into the hallway and slamming the door closed behind her. Terrified, she grabbed the phone receiver, but there was no dial tone. The cord had been pulled out of the socket. *Someone disconnected it!* Her panic rising, she pulled herself up onto her knees, her eyes darting around the hallway. *There was someone else in the house.* Picking up the cord, she scrambled to find the connecting socket, before jamming it back into the wall. This time, when she picked up the receiver, the dial tone was back. With a sense of relief, she moved her fingers to the dial when suddenly, everything went dark. Maria thrashed around, trying to throw off the person who was covering her eyes. The giggling returned; this time louder, reverberating in her ears. The more she thrashed, the more intense the giggling became. Eventually she was released. In a daze, she collapsed onto the stairs by the telephone stand. As her vision returned, she could see someone standing in front of her. It was a boy, around 12 years old. In raggedy, filthy clothes, with dirt on his face and wavy hair, matted with mud. He beamed at her, stifling his laughter through his grimy hand.

Maria's eyes widened in shock as she realised who he was. Someone she hadn't seen in years. Someone who three therapists had convinced her was only in her imagination. Someone she feared more than anything else in the world.

"Mr Piggy!"

He giggled.

"How are you here?"

The young boy, grinning from ear-to-ear, slowly walked forward. Maria was too stunned to move. He stopped right in front of her, both of them staring into each other's eyes. She noticed he hadn't aged a day. He was still the same, little boy she had always known. In the same clothes, with the same hair and that ridiculous laugh. As she looked into his deep, brown eyes, he punched her in the face and ran off, screaming "filthy bitch" before disappearing.

Maria touched her face. It was bleeding. How was any of this possible? With her heart in her throat, she reached over for the phone and dialled

999.

"Are you sure you don't want to stay here a little longer, darling? You've had an awful shock." Lady Braighton held on to her daughter's hand.

"You're lucky to be alive."

"Henry! Don't scare the girl."

"Well, it's bloody true. Anything could have happened. This is why you should be living here, where you're safe."

"I know you're both worried about me, but there's really no need. Hattie is out of danger now and apart from being a little embarrassed, I'm fine."

"Why are you embarrassed?" Elena asked.

"For calling the police, thinking there was an intruder in the flat."

"You weren't to know there wasn't. You find Hattie unconscious with marks on her chest and then fall over, scratching your face and not knowing if someone had tripped you up or not. I would have called the police under those circumstances."

"All of those officers scouring my flat for an intruder that wasn't there, while the paramedics were tending to Hattie."

Lady Braighton's eyes watered. "The poor dear must have been in so much pain to cause those marks on her chest. It must be terrifying to have a heart attack, it sounds awful. Thank goodness you were there to help her. Who knows if she'd have made it, if you hadn't been around."

"Don't upset yourself again dear. Hattie is out

of harm's way now, that's the main thing." Lord Braighton looked to his daughter. "What about the phone line being pulled out of the socket?"

"I must have kicked it out when I bounded into the hallway, in my haste to get to the phone. In the heat of the moment, I let my imagination get away from me. I suppose we didn't need to change the locks after all, Daddy."

"Nonsense. I should have organised that before you moved in anyway. You can never be too careful, especially in London." Lord Braighton moved towards the side of the room and poured himself a brandy.

"No more of that Henry, you've already had two."

"But I'm all flustered after everything that's happened."

"That's the excuse you've been using all week, it won't work anymore. Put the bottle down. I didn't marry a drunk."

"Yes dear." He placed the bottle back onto the antique sideboard and returned to his seat by the fireplace, sulking a little. "Are you sure you don't want to stay with us just a while longer?"

Maria was staring up at the large oil painting hanging on the wall. All three Braightons stood proudly in their finest attire. As a five-year-old, she remembered hating the many hours posing for the picture. Now, she smiled at the memory of just how close they were as a family. She turned to her father. "Thank you, Daddy, but I've already spent the past week here. The security firm you hired has finished the work and cleared out, so I'm good to go home."

"But you'll be on your own. Hattie is still at her sister's house recovering from her heart attack. It could be weeks until she's ready to go back to work."

"Actually, Mum, I've told her not to come back at all."

"What? Why?"

"She's well past retirement age and after what happened, I think she needs to live her own life from now on. She should savour every second, not be waiting on me and my needs. It took some convincing, you know how she gets, but in the end, she thanked me. Since her sister's husband died, she's been rattling around in that big old house in the Cotswolds and has hinted more than a few times that Hattie should move in with her. I'm sure the only reason she hadn't done it sooner is because of me. It's moments like this that make you realise just how precious life is. Every second of it."

"That's admirable darling, but what about you? Will you find a new maid?" Lady Braighton asked.

"I don't think so. I'd like to start doing things for myself. I've learned a lot of cooking skills from Hattie over the years and she's left me all of her cook books. I'm sure she knows all of those recipes by heart, anyway." Maria looked towards her muttering father.

"I'll be fine, Daddy. The doctor has given me some pills to calm the anxiety and I think it's time I got out into the world and made some friends of my own."

"You should be here, with your family."

"I'll be back so often, you'll probably still think that I'm living here," Maria chuckled. "I love you both very much, but it's time I took care of myself. I'm going to be ok. I promise."

"Hmmmm." Lord Braighton sank back into his chair, eyeing the brandy bottle again.

It was night time when Maria walked up to the front door of her flat. She was confronted with two new locks and a security panel. As she searched her bag for the code, she muttered to herself. "It's not the outside world I need to worry about."

She entered the numbers and unlocked the door, stepping into the hallway for the first time in a week. The same cold shiver she had felt then, returned.

Am I going crazy? Maria thought. *Mr Piggy was here, but how? He was just my silly imaginary friend from when I was a kid.*

She checked every room, but he was nowhere to be found. The medication she was given was working to shut him out, just as it had before. She walked into the bathroom and produced a medicine box from her handbag. She looked inside; there were enough pills to get her through the next month. What would she do then? She couldn't tell anyone Mr Piggy had returned, not even Doctor Sharma – he was too close to her family. If her parents found out, they would surely force her to move back into the manor.

Maria looked at herself in the mirror.

"You can get through this, one way or another, you can. You just need to do whatever it takes to make sure he doesn't return."

She filled a glass of water from the bathroom tap and popped one of the pills in her mouth. As she swallowed it, she stared at her reflection.

"Whatever it takes."

The Cracked Reflection is an introductory novella to REFRACTION - now available on Kindle and Paperback, worldwide from Amazon.

READ ON FOR A SNEAK PEEK FROM

REFRACTION

PROLOGUE

"Why is there a dinosaur in here?"

"Sorry, Doctor Padman - I mean Doctor Sharma - it must have followed me in."

"Please be more careful. We only have a few months before the soft launch and the last thing we need is a rogue microraptor attacking Stephen Fry."

"I'll remove it now."

"Please do." The doctor sat down and breathed a heavy sigh. "Oh, and get one of the tech team in here, will you? The dinosaurs are meant to be docile, not attacking everything in sight," he called to the young man who was now scurrying out of the room, dragging the raptor behind him, on a long catch-pole.

We'll never be finished in time, the doctor thought, cradling his head in his hands.

"You called?"

Padman looked up to see Lan Ying standing in front of him.

"How did you get here so fast?"

"I was on my way to speak to you, when I bumped into the new recruit wrestling with a microraptor."

"And why was he wrestling with it? Your team was supposed to have fixed that."

"Changing the digital code is taking longer than expected. We're working around the clock to find a solution."

Padman loosened his tense expression.

"I know you are and I'm extremely grateful, I'm just concerned because in a few months' time, families will be walking around these rooms. It needs to be safer than a trip to DisneyWorld."

"No hurricanes either then?"

"I'm serious, Lan Ying." Padman raised an eyebrow.

"I know, I'm sorry. Gallows humour, I guess. It's frustrating being on such a tight deadline. I understand why we can't employ any more people…"

"Look what happens when we do!" Padman indicated to the door and the intern who had just exited. Lan Ying chuckled.

"Even with all hands-on-deck, we are still struggling. Do you think we could push back the opening date a bit, like maybe another year?"

"A year? We're lucky the board agreed to a few months. If it were up to them, we'd be opening next week." Padman scoffed as he stood up.

The doctor led the way through the exhibition, continuing their conversation while he inspected the room. "The museum is looking great, everything is coming together and most importantly, everything works. These are just tweaks; the final few checks before we open and finally go public with all of this."

"Do you know how long that check-list is?"

"I know, but we're creating – scratch that – have created, the impossible. Soon, everyone in the world will want to come here and marvel at what we've achieved. I am so proud of you, the whole team in fact. What we've built together is nothing short of miraculous."

Lan Ying smiled. "Thank you, that really does mean a lot. I promise we'll fix the dinosaur problem as soon as possible."

"I know you will and I know how tired you all must be. Just keep pushing that bit further and in a few months' time, we can all get a good night's sleep."

"That would be great. I feel like I haven't slept in weeks."

"I actually haven't!"

They both laughed as they neared the exit. A woman was pacing back and forth in front of the door, chuntering to herself. "I'll never let go, Jack. I'll never let go, Jack. I'll never let go, Jack."

"Why is she doing that?"

"That's actually what I wanted to talk to you about. We don't yet have enough dialogue for the character."

"It shouldn't be a problem to programme that in though."

Lan Ying shifted, nervously. "Of course, no it shouldn't, but, well, Felix informed me that Kate Winslet will be in our recording studio next week and I just wondered…"

"No! Certainly not."

"But I think it would add to the realism."

"Look around, everything here is a perfect re-creation. We have the voice of Rose on file, use that like you would any other character. The last thing we need are Hollywood agents wanting a cut from every actor we've replicated."

"Good point. I was just excited at the prospect of meeting her."

Padman smiled. "I'm taking Kate to The Ivy for dinner, after the recording. Why don't you come along with us?"

Lan Ying beamed. "Seriously?"

"Yes. You've earned it." Padman smiled. "As long as those dinosaurs are under control by then."

"Believe me, they will be!"

Chapter 1

San Francisco

Abby was running as fast as she could. The young girl couldn't remember why, but with her heart pumping, the quickening of her breath and the fear that coursed through her body; all her senses knew it was the right thing to do. She was being chased. Abby swerved around the trees of the darkened forest, her mind racing and not knowing where she was nor how she could escape from her unknown assailant.

It was the noise that first alerted her to the ocean, and as she neared the edge of a cliff, the sound of the waves could be heard, crashing on the rocks far below. If Abby stopped now, she would be giving herself to the Shadow Man, a prospect that filled her with even more fear than falling into the moonlit ocean below.

The girl continued running, and without thinking twice, as she neared the edge of the cliff, she pushed off from the side and jumped high into the air, much higher than she ever would have thought possible. She felt as light as a feather, her white nightgown billowing ever so gently, as if pushing her farther up towards the stars. Abby felt as if she were flying and ascending higher into the night sky. She glanced back to the cliff edge, where the dark shape of a man with burning red eyes was standing, motionless, staring directly at her. Abby was safe. He couldn't follow her up here.

As she rose higher, a gust of wind caught her long, dark hair, blowing it in front of her face. Scrambling to clear her view, she felt a jolt in her stomach as gravity kicked in, causing her to drop out of the sky. She was falling fast now, plunging towards the ocean below with no way of slowing her descent. Panic surged through her as she kicked her legs violently; a futile attempt to propel herself back to safety. It didn't work. She tumbled clumsily through the air, her young body falling downwards until her face was mere metres from the crashing water.

Abby bolted upright and let out a small scream as she scrambled to untangle herself from the duvet and blankets wrapped around her. She was back in her bedroom, lit only by the light of a small lava lamp at her side. As she readjusted to the familiar surroundings, a second, ghost-like girl also sat upright and occupied the same space as Abby, now staring at the trembling reflection of herself in the lamp.

The bedroom door burst open and the harsh light from the hallway filled the room as her flustered mother came in to check on her. Out of breath, wiping sleep from her eyes and visibly shaken, Shira pulled her daughter close to her in an embrace which comforted both of them.

"My darling, are you OK?"

"I was being chased, I fell and, and —"

"It's all right, it was just a bad dream. You're safe now. I'm here to look after you. No-one will chase you while I'm here, or they'll get this." Shira clenched her fist and shook it comically in the air.

A small tear escaped Abby's eye; a tear brought on from the fear she had felt, the relief that the dream had ended, and the comfort brought by her mother. She wiped her eyes, smiled, and settled back down into bed.

After a long while, with her mother gently stroking her hair, Abby finally fell back to sleep.

***

Bedford

"The most upsetting part is that she won't even look at me." Terrell was walking along the school corridor with his best friend, Cody, talking about the same girl he had been obsessing about since before he knew what the word 'obsession' meant.

"I've seen her look at you, mate."

"Really?" Terrell's face lit up.

"Quite often, actually, but it's more of a scowl." Cody pulled a face, mimicking the look of disgust from the object of Terrell's affections.

"Great. Thanks for that." Terrell's shoulders returned to their slumped position as they continued through the school. "I'm crazy about her, the least she could do is be nice to me. The occasional smile, asking how I am, leading to us grabbing a slice of pizza together, working on some homework in the library and then, when the time is right, she leans over for a kiss —"

A bag swung into Terrell's back, snapping him out of his temporary lapse in concentration.

"Stop dreaming, mate. She's never going to fancy you. You're a geek and she's . . . well, she's Lindsay Coppard — the hottest girl in school."

Terrell straightened himself up and looked at Cody.

"Dreaming's preferable to the reality of her hating my guts."

"Can you blame her? You did puke over her bag in chemistry."

"That was in year seven. How was I supposed to know that burning sulphur was going to make me hurl? Can people really still hold that against me? It's been six years."

The boys turned into the lunch-hall, where a group of girls spotted them.

"Hey, Pukey!" the tallest of the girls called as Terrell passed by, eliciting a cascade of muffled giggles from her friends.

Cody hugged Terrell's shoulder and quickly ushered him away.

"Mate, don't take this the wrong way, but maybe girls just aren't for you?"

***

Yorkshire

Daylight was breaking through the clouds as Jake donned his filthy, worn-out wellington boots. Yet another long day lay ahead, tending to his land and livestock. Upper Malham Farm had been passed down through many generations; it had been his father's dying wish that Jake continue in the family footsteps. His father had always been a strong, proud man and on seeing him frail and failing as he took his last breaths in a hospital bed, Jake had held his hand and agreed to take over the farm. Being an only child and the last remaining family member, there was really no-one else who could.

That had been two years ago, and now this remote farm in northern England had become his prison. The prospect of doing this for the rest of his life filled him with dread. At twenty-six years old, he rarely ventured away from the farm and his computer had become his only window to the outside world.

Agriculture was no longer a booming business and the low turnover meant he could only afford to employ a skeleton staff. Jake worked seven days a week; hard, relentless, tiring, physical work. He wished for a different life but could see no way out of his current one.

The young farmer's boots sloshed through the soft mud. The cool air of a new day chilled his face as he made his way across the field. In front of him was a battered, old tractor. Jake pulled himself up into the driver's seat and stared through the windscreen.

The sun was rising behind the old birch trees in the distance, casting wild patterns over the valley floor and the huge puddles of water on the track in front of him. A flock of birds soared through the air, moving in perfect formation, disappearing towards the horizon. They left behind an eerie silence.

Still half-asleep, Jake's mind began to wander and he closed his eyes, breathing in the moment. A few seconds later, his body was slumped over the steering wheel, fast asleep, yet a ghostlike version of him was still sitting upright in the cabin, eyes open and staring straight ahead.

***

Kent

Ryder was the illegitimate child of Lord and Lady Braighton's only daughter, Maria. After a near-fatal accident in Afghanistan, Ryder had been medically discharged from the army. Wheelchair-bound, he was finding it difficult to adjust to everyday life, especially having no money to support himself. He hoped his estranged family would be able to offer some financial stability, at least for the immediate future. His mother had passed away some years before and he hadn't been back to Braighton Manor since.

Ryder waited patiently in the sitting-room. The name belied the room's grandiosity. Priceless works of art adorned the walls, but the one that really stood out was the oil painting of his mother, positioned above the open, stone fireplace.

Heavy footsteps echoed in the distance; the louder the sound, the closer the footsteps and the stronger Ryder's heartbeat. The pounding in his chest seemed to match the pace of the steps, until they stopped right outside the room. There was a pause where no sound could be heard for a few seconds, then a creaking of hinges announced Lord Braighton's arrival.

Carrying a stern look on his face, the lord walked towards Ryder and held out his hand.

"Ah, Ryder, so good of you to come. It's been too long since you were here last." Lord Braighton shook his grandson's hand and then stood back to survey the wheelchair. "I see the army's left its mark on you, but as they say, 'what doesn't kill us makes us stronger', and all that."

The two men regarded each other in an awkward silence before Lord Braighton walked across to the antique sideboard; his Italian leather shoes tapping on the mahogany floor beneath him. He fixed himself a neat brandy without offering one to his guest.

Ryder opened his mouth to speak but no sound came out. With a dry throat, he swallowed hard in an attempt to regain composure.

"Good afternoon, sir. I'm sorry to arrive unannounced. I realise we haven't spoken since Mum died. I'm sorry for not keeping in touch. I hope being here today isn't an inconvenience?"

"Not at all. Good of you to come, good of you to

come."

There was another awkward silence. Both men glanced around the stately room in a bid to avoid the other's gaze. The lord drained his glass as both men's eyes came to rest on the painting above the fireplace. A pang of emotion hit Ryder's chest. He hated himself for coming here, but he was desperate. So desperate, in fact, that he was about to ask for help from the person he believed was responsible for his mother's death.

Continue the story in Refraction – now available on Kindle and paperback, exclusively from Amazon, worldwide.

ENTER THE REFRACTED WORLD

https://linktr.ee/terryjgeo

www.refractedworld.com

www.twitter.com/terryjgeo

Instagram: @terryjgeo

www.facebook.com/refractedworld

ABOUT THE AUTHOR

Born in Derbyshire, raised in Yorkshire, resides in London.

Terry Geo wrote and directed his first play at age eleven. At sixteen, he started work in television, writing scripts and becoming the youngest director in the country. After a short stint in a boyband, Terry went back to writing, editing two national publications. He toured the world as an actor, moved to London and in 2017, wrote and directed an award-nominated musical for the London stage.

In 2019, Terry published his debut novel, Refraction to critical acclaim. The Cracked Reflection is the introductory novella to that story.

ACKNOWLEDGEMENTS

I first need to thank my husband. I receive a lot of love and support from him on a daily basis. Writing is a solitary profession and he understands my need for absolute quiet when I'm writing, but as that is not always possible when we're both working from home, noise-cancelling headphones are always on hand.

I will bounce ideas off him, he's my beta, alpha and proof reader and is the person I turn to (literally, his desk is behind mine) for every idea I have and decision I make. Without Ken, I wouldn't be a published author, I would still be aspiring to achieve my dreams and goals. For that, I owe him everything.

I'd also like to thank my brother, Max. He's the second person I always turn to (not literally) and the second reader of every story I write. There are always things I miss through tired or word-blinded eyes. No one can be their own editor and I'm thankful to be able to call on him.

My best friend Michael is a beta reader for me as well as my new friend Melinda. Both have been great support networks and I'm extremely happy they both offered to read my pre-published work without me having to ask them – and worry it was an inconvenience!

My Mum always comes to mind when I'm

thanking people. She has always supported me in everything I have done, although I don't believe she truly understands the worlds I create. She's not a geek like I am, doesn't follow pop-culture and has never been a fan of the science fiction genre, but she does enjoy the interactions of the characters I create. Whenever I write, in whatever setting, I spend months perfecting dialogue. Humans have and always will interact with each other in familiar and relatable ways. If I get it right, I hope to be able to entertain anyone with my stories, regardless of the genre or setting.

Along the social media journey, I discovered the online writing community. There, I have made many new friends - all writers in their own right and yet, many of them willing to give help and advice to each other. A constant exchange of support and ideas which has been invaluable.

Published life has been an exciting, elating and sometimes frustrating experience. Writing is a difficult profession – self-published life, I would say, even more so. You are not just a writer, you are also an editor, a marketeer, a salesperson, a designer... You do everything from the first word to the final sale. You have no publisher to tell you what works and what doesn't, you can only use your own judgement and test the market to see what works and what doesn't.

I spend a long time perfecting my craft. I want my words to entertain and resonate with people. I love hearing back from those who read my books and want to share their thoughts and feelings on the characters I've created. For me, being a novelist is about sharing a story that once only lived in my head and is now available to anyone who flips through the pages of my books. Visiting the worlds I create and meeting the characters I have given life to.

Books give us the freedom to expand our minds more than any other entertainment medium and to share that experience with others. This isn't a lucrative profession, but it is a fulfilling one.

Thanks for reading!

Terry

Printed in Great Britain
by Amazon

67490165R00078